A FINE BASKET OF FISH

a Beatrice Sterling novel
by Barry Scott Will

A Fine Basket of Fish
© 2013 Barry Scott Will

ISBN 978-1-940919-00-3 (EPUB)
ISBN 978-1-940919-01-0 (MOBI)
ISBN 978-1-940919-02-7 (PRINT)

Published in the United States of America
Valutivity Press
www.valutivitypress.com

Cover art by Ashton Leigh Will

Printed by CreateSpace

To Karen, Xander, Ashton, and Alexa. Thank you for supporting and inspiring me.
 - *Barry Scott Will*

ONE

"Name?"

"Beatrice Sterling."

"...You don't look like a Beatrice."

I smiled through my beard. "The doc who scryed me missed an important detail and my parents had already bonded the name..." I shrugged in the practiced, nonchalant way showing I didn't really care. It kept people from pressing the point, even if it wasn't true.

The guard dismissed the situation with a grunt. "What do you want?"

"I'm responding to an ad this morning about a job."

"Oh, yeah. You want the third floor. Room 316. Lifts are around the corner." The ogre vaguely waved me away to the right.

I grinned at her, which she didn't see, and headed for the lifts. The building was a standard ogre-sized tower in the commercial center of Fisk. From the outside it appeared shabbier than the surrounding towers and definitely needed a new coat of paint and cleaner windows. I didn't have high hopes for the lifts, and, as I suspected, the lift operator was just an apprentice. Any office building unwilling to spring for at least adepts to run the lifts wasn't going to be a great source of income. But I needed the work, so I gritted my teeth and walked forward.

"I need a lift to the third floor."

The youngster glared at me for daring to interrupt the determined destruction of his fingernails. He transferred the glare to one of the metal platters nearby and levitated it into a lift tube. I stepped on and felt the stasis field grab my legs. I clenched my hip and back muscles against what was coming and the little twerp threw me half a story past three and then dropped me just as quickly to a little below the right level.

Clamping down on the sudden nausea, I clambered up onto the floor, avoiding looking down at the twelve lengths of empty air under me. The apprentice barely let me get off before he zipped the lift back down. I sighed and looked around for room signs and followed them to 316. A small plaque beside the door advertised "J. Cristof, Public Services."

I walked into a waiting room full of various levels of mercenary grunge. I spied a seat between an ogre and what might have been a troll or a human with bad hygiene; it's hard to tell the difference sometimes. I didn't even make it across the room before a side door opened and an elf stepped out and announced in a loud, squeaky voice, "Beatrice Sterling!"

I thought how crazy it was there was another Betty Sterling here to apply for the job, but no one moved or even glanced at me or the elf. I looked down at the elf and he looked right back up at me and said, "Mr. Sterling?" I dumbly nodded and followed him down a short hall to a small room with a round table and four chairs, one occupied.

A tall man, with a close-cropped beard and brown hair tied back, stood and greeted me. "Ah, Mr. Sterling. Joshua Cristof. We've been expecting you."

I shook his hand, warily. "OK, you've got me. How do you know me, how did you know I was coming, and why did you call me in right away?"

He chuckled. "I know prophecy is an inexact art, but I have certain advantages. It helps me arrange my day."

"Yeah, even the weather scryers can't tell you if it's raining without looking outside first." I was unconvinced. "So if you knew I was coming, what's with the waiting room full of people?"

"Other associates. For other jobs." His smile never wavered and I swear his eyes even twinkled. "But why don't we talk about what I want you to do?"

I just sat and stared at him; I thought I was immune to surprise.

Cristof talked right over my silence. "I specialize in providing services for people in trouble. I prefer to hire others to do the actual work, under close supervision, of course. It has come to my attention there is a little problem in some villages along the Sea of Arran. I'll give you 1,000 marks in advance, and another thousand when the job is complete."

I was stunned. Two thousand marks...I could take a year off with that, even after expenses. Still..."I need to know the details before I make a commitment."

"Certainly. In short, there are a number of fishing villages along the northwest coast that specialize in catching a certain type of fish—bluefin...ever hear of it?" I shook my head. "Well, trust me when I say it is considered a delicacy and sells for a generous amount. A reduction in bluefin production has created a considerable hardship among the people of those villages. They have appealed to me for help and I'm sending you!" He finished with a flourish and a smile as though this were the best news delivered in quite some time.

"I'm...lost. I thought I was coming in for an interview for muscle. That's what I am. I'm the blunt instrument. People don't hire me to help other people, they hire me to hurt them. It's what I do. Now you want to send me off on a...fishing expedition?"

"As you say, Mr. Sterling. You're a blunt instrument. I believe this job will require a blunt instrument. I'm convinced you're the right man for the job."

"I'm flattered, Mr. Cristof, but I'm not an investigator. I don't ask questions. I'm the person that gets sent in when the questions have already been asked and the answers were wrong."

"I'm aware of your past history, Mr. Sterling." Cristof absently patted a folder beside him, the first I had noticed it. "It's my belief it's time for a change of pace. You've been working for, shall we say, more selfish reasons. This is a chance to...redeem yourself. Do something for the greater good. I guarantee you'll find the work more rewarding than shaking down recalcitrant debtors and the like."

I stared at the folder on the table. It felt like the weight of my life suddenly pressed against me and I could feel a hot flush building in my face. I didn't like the feeling. "I'm sorry, Mr. Cristof. I think you're way off. I don't need to atone for my actions. I do my job and let other people worry about the mess. I don't fix messes."

Cristof pulled the folder to him and flipped it open. "Beatrice Marie Sterling," he read. "Born in 2213 Common Year, making you...30 years of age. Doctor told your parents you were a girl, which is how you ended up with your name, despite obviously not being a girl. Bonded by that name prior to your birth, so, no luck getting a name change afterward. History of difficulty in school—mostly fistfights, it appears."

"Yeah, well, when you're a boy with a name like Betty, certain people think it's funny until you bloody their nose."

"They think it's funny, or you find it embarrassing?" Cristof's eyes bored into me, then he looked back down at the papers in front of him. "Entered Uvorth Martial Academy at age 12 and trained under Master Jorrargh...an ogre?"

I nodded. "Yeah. Most of the students were ogres. I learned what it meant to be on the wrong side of 'pick on someone your own size.'"

Cristof chuckled. "I can imagine. Graduated with honors, though, at age 22. Been living on your own since, working as a freelance mercenary. Parents still living, as well as two brothers and a sister, but no other family. A long string of jobs...mostly trying to squeeze blood from a stone."

"It pays the bills." I shrugged.

"For a one-room walkup near Tannytown."

"I'm frugal. And the smell keeps the bugs away."

Cristof grinned at me. "So you're happy with your life?"

The flush that had been building went full bloom and I swallowed. Under his gaze, I suddenly found I couldn't lie. "No." It was barely above a whisper.

Cristof closed the folder, somehow making it sound as though it had slammed shut, though it was just paper. "Come work for me, Mr. Sterling. It's better work. It pays more. And, who knows, maybe working *for* someone else rather than *on* someone else will make you feel better about you." He pulled out a pouch and slid it across to me. "Look up Lilah Burkah in the town of Darfa on the west coast of the Sea of Arran. Here's one thousand marks. Hire some help and transportation. Go forth and do some good." He smiled at me again.

I reached in the bag and felt the magic charge on the marks. Each one tingled as a small spell communicated its authenticated amount to me. Maybe it was time to move up in the world.

"Oh," Cristof said, "there's just one more little detail..."

TWO

"So you took the job."

"Uh-huh." I looked across the table at Jewels. My sometimes partner had a quizzical expression on her tiny face.

"This is the weirdest thing you've ever signed on for, Betty, and that's saying something."

"Weirder than the potion-maker? I still have strange dreams from that one."

"Okay, maybe not that weird." Jewels sighed, "Go ahead, lay it out for me."

"Are you signing up too?" I asked.

"You didn't bring me to lunch because you like my company. Besides, I want a piece of that action."

"But I do like your company, Jewels."

"You're a flatterer, Betty, and not very good at it. You're going to need a good technician on this trip, and I'm the best one you know."

"Thanks, Jewels, I really appreciate your offer to help."

"It's not an offer. I expect to be paid and we will sign a contract stating such. Now, stop the platitudes and give me the details so I know how much I'm going to charge you." She rested her elbows on her knees and her head on her fists and stared at me with her big, lavender eyes.

"OK. On the Sea of Arran are a lot of small villages. They are part of Glomwill ..."

"Excuse me." I looked up at the waiter who had been working the counter and now hovered over us. "Yes?" I asked.

"Could you tell your fairy not to sit on the table?" Oh no, I thought, here we go.

"I am an ELF, not a fairy!" Jewels had jumped straight to apoplexy. "See? No WINGS! And I'm not HIS, I'm MINE. Got that? And I will sit where I can see because you idiots don't have proper seating for elves. Come on, Betty. Let's go somewhere else!"

"But...we haven't gotten our food yet."

"I'm not hungry anymore." Jewels was already halfway to the door, under the gaze of every other customer in the place. I apologetically shoved a few marks toward the waiter and hurried after. Jewels was moving fast, despite her short legs. I know she's enhancing, but I don't know what to do about it.

I finally caught her at the end of the street, where she was waiting for a line of floaters to pass. We stood silently together until the street cleared and then stood a little longer.

"So," I said to break the silence. "Where are we going?" She didn't answer, just stood with her arms crossed staring at the empty street. "Maybe we should go and see Sam?" I suggested. "I probably should have included him anyway."

"OK," she said and headed away to the right in the direction of Ogretown.

"Wouldn't it be faster to hire a floater?" I asked as I hurried to keep pace. She was definitely enhancing. That or she was really working those little legs.

"I need to walk." She looked back over her shoulder at me, "And you look like you're out of shape."

"Hey! Can't we slow down?"

~

Fisk, primary center of business for The Fisk Company, is a sizable city. And, in any sizable city, there will be an Ogretown. Ogres are twice the size of humans and need homes and shops and bars, and everything else, to match. Big public buildings like the one where I met Cristof are built to ogre scale, but the only other place where ogres really fit in, is Ogretown.

Sam lives in a small (for an ogre) row house on Basin Street not far from the harbor. Jewels and I arrived mid-afternoon, trying to ignore the unfriendly glances from the giant, tusked ogres hurrying up and down the street. I pounded the doorknocker and hoped Sam was home.

"Who is it?" Sam's voice always surprises me. I expect ogres to have deep, guttural voices to go along with their tusks and brutish faces. But Sam had a soft lilt, almost musical. Which only makes sense; he plays five instruments and makes his living playing gigs around town.

"It's Betty and Jewels. Can we come in for a few minutes?"

The door opened and I was staring up at Sam's green, hairless face. "With you two it is never 'a few minutes.'" Sam smiled, a non-pleasant expression for an ogre. "Please come in. I have the night free and was planning a quiet evening at home."

"I hate to disturb you," I apologized. Sam snorted, but I plowed on. "I got a job this morning. I've already hired Jewels..."

"We haven't signed a contract yet!"

"...and we could use your help as well."

Sam escorted us in and invited us to sit. He sat, leaned back, crossed his legs, and steepled his fingers in front of himself. "Yes, a few minutes indeed. Go on, tell me more."

I shifted uncomfortably in my chair. While a good armchair for an ogre, for me it was as big as a loveseat and two lengths off the ground. Not that the height mattered, since my feet barely reached the edge. I felt like an infant.

"I've been hired to investigate problems in a fishing community on the Sea of Arran. The job pays 2,000 marks and I want to hire you and Jewels to help me out."

"Investigate? You?" Sam interrupted. "You are not an investigator, Betty. You are the tool used by investigators."

I bristled at Sam's blunt assessment. "I know my limitations, Sam." My tone was dry. "That's why I want to take you. You're better at asking questions. Once we get the information we need, you point me to who needs to be taught a lesson and I teach it. Jewels backs us both up with tech."

"The Sea of Arran, you said?" I nodded and Sam got up and rummaged in a drawer for a map. He spread it out on his table, but I didn't bother to get up and go look. My eyes would barely clear the top edge. Jewels, on the other hand, quickly levitated over and peered at the map along with Sam.

"That is in Glomwill Holdings' area. Tenth Hold if this map is still accurate. Why would a Fisk Company rep send you down to Glomwill?"

"This guy isn't Fisk. He says he's an independent."

Jewels blurted out, "Hey! You didn't tell me you weren't working for Fisk!"

"You didn't give me a chance before you had your fit in the restaurant. Look, does it matter? Isn't it better if we stay out of inter-corp squabbles?"

Sam stared at me. "Do you want to get involved if some start-up has designs on the corporations?"

"If he's trying a takeover, why would he be spending money to help out?"

Sam slowly shook his head, "I will not lecture you on economics, but strengthening the enemy of your enemy is sound business practice. After they are finished with each other, the victor will be weak and vulnerable."

"There hasn't been a hostile takeover in decades," I protested.

"History cannot predict the future, Betty. But...I agree it is unlikely anyone from Fisk would be sending you to Glomwill with nefarious intentions. I am not entirely sanguine with the hiring; however, I think we can put that aside for the nonce. Continue with your explanation."

"OK, like I said, there are some villages on the Sea of Arran. Part of this Tenth Hold, if your map is right. They survive on fishing—some type of local fish called a bluefin." Sam's eyebrow went up. "The fish are disappearing. Last season there were plenty, now the nets keep coming up empty or close to it. Mr. Cristof, the guy who hired me, doesn't think this is natural and wants me to go find out what's happening and put a stop to it. He specifically mentioned I should hire as much extra help as I need and paid me a thousand in advance. We'll get another thousand when we finish the job."

"Well, it certainly seems cut and dried. I am just not sure it will be simple. Determining the cause of disappearing fish...there could be any number of reasons. Ecological changes, intrusion of some new predator, and so on. There does not need to be any nefarious goings-on to account for the problem. In fact, I do not see how any other boats could be out there fishing without the locals knowing what is happening. I can see how this is a big problem for the villages and, probably, for Glomwill Holdings as a whole. Bluefin is quite a delicacy around Ilanerra, and Gorsj as well. I know in the markets here in Fisk it sells for something over a mark per pound."

I whistled. As much water as there is on Berrea, fishing is a major occupation all over and most fish sell for about a tenth of that. "All right, now I know why they need help. And if somebody IS out there catching up all the fish, that explains why Cristof is sending me—somebody will need to convince the other fishermen to go elsewhere. And it also explains the money, there's definitely a lot of it riding on this."

Jewels piped up, "So, when are we leaving?"

Sam turned to his desk and grabbed his memory slate. It took him a moment to establish psychic contact with the slate, then, with his eyes unfocused, he said, "I have a show tomorrow night and another next week. I can cancel the one next week, if need be, but I should fulfill my commitment for the show tomorrow. I could leave the morning after. That would be the fifteenth."

"OK," I said. "That gives me a day to pack. How are we getting there?"

"We can't use The Tube," Jewels said, "on account of Sam not fitting in one. That would be the fastest way there. I guess we could hire a floater, it shouldn't take more than half a day to drive, should it?"

Sam had put down his slate and was looking at his map again. "I would say closer to a full day to drive there. But, when we arrive, will we not need a boat? We could just hire a boat and travel that way."

I sighed. "That makes sense, Sam. But...ugh, I hate boats."

THREE

The morning of the fifteenth dawned bright and clear. I could tell because I was up before dawn—not my favorite time to be out of bed. I had spent the previous day making sure I had all my equipment in order and hiring an ogre-sized boat.

I reached Fisk's main harbor a little after the sun had cleared the horizon and headed to Bluewater Marina where I had booked the charter. Sam and Jewels were already there and Sam was explaining the ship's drive system to Jewels.

"There are propellers attached to rotating platforms extending below the boat. A propulsion spell on each propeller spins it, providing thrust. The helmsman steers by rotating the propeller platforms, changing the direction of thrust. The steerage links are all mechanical, so the only tech needed is for the propellers."

"But," Jewels protested, "why don't they just put a propulsion spell on the boat itself, like with floaters?"

"Floaters are small and only have to move through air. My assumption is the weight of the boat and the resistance of the water make attaching propulsion directly to the boat prohibitive. Spinning a propeller is far more efficient and requires less concentration from the pilot than the effort to move something that large through water. But, if you really want to know, you can talk to the captain." Jewels grabbed her duffel and strode across the passerelle, an eager look on her face that presaged the captain having a time entertaining her questions.

The boat was built for ogres, which meant it was alot bigger than what I, or especially Jewels, needed. But it had living quarters on board so we wouldn't need to stop along the way. Sam hefted his duffel and a big box. I raised my eyebrow at him in lieu of a question.

"Provisions for the trip," he answered.

"Feeding us is part of the charter," I told him.

"Forgive me," he said, "but rarely do humans provide enough food to actually satiate an ogre." He breezed past me and onto the ship, which suddenly didn't seem as large with him on board.

"Excuse me, sir." I looked up to see the captain hailing me from the deck. Despite the size of the boat being fit for ogres, the crew of four were all human. "We're ready to cast off as soon as you and your friends have your gear stowed."

I thanked him, hefted my duffel, gritted my teeth and picked my way over to the deck. My stomach was already doing flip-flops. Sam needn't have worried about food—he could just eat my share.

~

The run southeast along the Ilanerra coast would take, according to Captain Spanner, about three days running day and night. He and his crew would work in shifts to keep the boat moving and otherwise leave the three of us to fend for ourselves. The boat had two guest staterooms and Jewels had already co-opted the larger for herself, which seemed unfair to me as she needed only about one-eighth the space. That left Sam and me to put our things in the smaller stateroom with the bunk beds. I took the top—the thought of all five lengths of him sleeping over me made me feel a little claustrophobic.

I stowed my bag in a locker under the lower bunk, then climbed up, lay down and tried not to think about the movement of the ship. Through the bulkheads I could hear Captain Spanner calling out orders to the crew to get underway. The boat vibrated with the movement of the propellers and we slid away from the pier. Remarkably, as speed picked up, the boat began to smooth out and the constant rocking motion stopped—or, at least, slowed enough so I didn't notice it.

Within about a half-hour my stomach had settled enough for me to go looking for Sam and Jewels. They were together in the main salon, sitting around the lone table. Or, Sam was sitting around it, Jewels was sitting on it. She laughed as I came into the room, "Your skin was almost as green as Sam's! We thought you were going to spend the entire voyage in your bunk."

"So did I," I grimaced. If my normally dark skin had turned green, I had been sicker than I thought.

"For how long did you charter the boat, Betty?" Sam interjected.

"One month. It cost about five hundred of those

thousand marks I've already been paid, but, like you said, Sam, we're probably going to need a boat while we're there."

"Very good." Sam had maps spread out in front of him. "According to you, we are to see a Lilah Burkah in Darfa. I assume she is the Director of the Hold. We will need to begin by not only getting the director's approval to conduct operations in her area, but also thoroughly questioning her about the problems the Hold has been experiencing."

"So we know what we need to do. Now we just have to sit around for three days until we get there." Jewels sighed. "I still think we should have rented a floater. Anyone want to play cards?"

~

I spent most of the trip in bed trying to rest as my seasickness gradually got worse. Running through the Durgah Straights wasn't bad most of the time, but whenever the seas would kick up, the boat would slow and the rocking motion would become more pronounced. By the time we arrived off Darfa, I was sick and tired. Literally. I was sick, and I was tired from not getting enough sleep. Jewels was right—we should have just taken a floater overland and rented a boat locally.

We pulled into the harbor at Darfa shortly after noon. As I observed the small skiffs and fishing boats, I figured maybe having a bigger boat was the right choice after all. There wasn't an ogre-sized vessel anywhere and the boats I saw looked incredibly unsafe to me, rocking and swaying in the swell of the ocean. There were no piers capable of docking a ship our size, so after some tells with the harbormaster, Captain Spanner made anchor just inside the breakwater and sent us ashore in the ship's tender.

A crewman ran us in to a rocky beach away from the bustle of the main port. We hauled ourselves over the gunwale and headed up to a street running along the beach. There were few floaters on the street, most people were on foot. They generally ignored us—only a few even glanced in our direction.

"They don't seem surprised to see an ogre, do they, Sam?" I was a little shocked. Small-town people usually shy away from an ogre.

"We are not that far from Gorsj." Sam somehow managed to get the guttural bass into the name of the ogre homeland, despite his soft voice. "There are probably traveling ogres moving through here frequently, and there may even be a small Ogretown. Which would be wonderful, otherwise I will be sleeping on the ship."

I spotted a policewoman on the opposite side of the street, and crossed over to her. "Excuse me, we're looking for directions..."

"Yes, sir, new in town?" Her voice was flat and bored and she clearly didn't care if we were new or not.

"We're looking for Lilah Burkah. Is she the Hold Director?"

Her eyes went flat and her voice became hostile. "Two blocks that way," she pointed, "turn left into town and keep walking until you see the Hold Sigil. That's the Hold House." She continued glaring at us as I thanked her and we headed off in the direction she indicated.

The town was old and there was a certain miasma that hung in the air—a feeling of hopelessness mixed with the tang of salt water and the general fishy odor that permeates all small seaside villages. One bright point were the buildings. Many older towns had wooden buildings darkened with age, giving them a gloomy look as though they sucked light from the air around them. The buildings here in Darfa were whitewashed plaster and constant exposure to the salty air near the sea had kept them white. They reflected light, making the town appear bright and sparkling, in stark contrast to the mood of the people as they plodded about their chores.

"There isn't a lot of tech in this town." Jewels was looking everywhere but where she was walking; people had to keep jumping out of her way, some not quite in time as elves aren't exactly eye-level for a human. Jewels seemed not to notice or care about the occasional bump. "There's hardly any floaters, and the harbor was full of sailboats. I don't see any public tell stations and that policewoman was carrying a baton, but no wand. And there's a shopping district, but no tech shops." Jewels paused for a moment, "A tech could make a killing here."

"Thinking of settling down and becoming an honest merchant?" I kidded her. She narrowed her eyes and stuck out her tongue at me, but didn't reply. She was right though. Darfa looked like a town from the last age, before tech became widespread. I felt uncomfortable. I was born and raised in a big city and I was used to the bustle of lots of tech. I hoped I had brought enough with me; I wouldn't be able to replace anything that broke down.

The local Hold House was a three-story affair several blocks from the harbor. It had the mark of the Hold Director next to the door and was distinctly human-sized. "Sorry, Sam." I really was apologetic; corporate offices should be built to accommodate his people.

"It is quite all right, Betty," Sam was affable. "I will wait out here and partake of the wonderful odor of rotting fish from the harbor." He grinned.

I gave him a rueful smile and headed inside with Jewels at my heels. A man at a desk eyed us as we approached. "Name and business?" He asked.

"Beatrice Sterling and Jewels. We are working for a Mr. Cristof. He said Lilah Burkah would be expecting us."

"Just a moment." The man seemed suspicious, but grabbed a nearby tell and focused his attention on it and said, "Mary Kyle" in the sort of sing-song voice most people use when talking to tech. In a moment the tell had established telepathic contact with his subject and he went glassy-eyed as he communicated with her. After a brief mental conversation, he came to and put down the tell. "Go down this hall and through the last door on the left. Mrs. Kyle will show you in to the Director."

As we walked down the hall, I noted the walls weren't made of wood, but of some kind of pebbly stone. I stopped and took a closer look and saw the walls were full of shells. Jewels was noticing it as well. "This is crazy!" She said, probably a little too loudly as people inside open offices looked up as we passed. "They don't make everything out of this, do they?"

"Actually, yes, we do." An older woman standing at the last door in the hall was looking at us with a bemused expression. "It's a type of rock that forms along the shoreline and is mostly ground-down shells. It's soft and easier to quarry than regular rock. We call it coquina."

"Mrs. Kyle, I presume." I extended a hand.

"Yes. You are the help Joshua sent?"

"I'm Beatrice Sterling. This is Jewels, our tech. The third member of our team, Sam, is outside. He couldn't fit inside comfortably."

"He's an ogre." Jewels added.

"Ah, I see. We do have a small Ogretown, but not many ogres pass through, and there are only a handful that live here. I'm afraid we don't build our public offices to suit. Come on in, Director Burkah will see you momentarily." She gestured us to chairs in her office.

We had only been sitting a few minutes when a tell on the desk beeped and Mrs. Kyle ushered us into the Director's office.

"A cat!" Jewels hissed under her breath. For someone who is as sensitive as Jewels, she's awfully insensitive about others.

Trolls aren't related to cats, but there is a superficial resemblance, with the fine fur that covers their bodies and the slightly protruding muzzle and large, almond-shaped eyes. Of course, most trolls in human communities don't take good care of themselves and they end up looking like hairy people who don't bathe often. Maybe that's on purpose, since they don't like being called 'cats.' I hoped Director Burkah hadn't heard, but I doubted it. Troll ears are sharp.

She didn't display any reaction. As she came around the desk I noted her fur was light—almost invisible—and she had big, golden eyes. "I'm so glad to meet you," she said extending her hand. She had long nails and a firm grip. Her palms were warm and the fur covering them was soft. I realized I was getting distracted and tried to focus on her. "I'm Lilah Burkah, Director of this Hold. Thank you for coming."

"I'm still a little confused about why we're here, Miss Burkah. Mr. Cristof only said the local fishing is drying up, but he didn't give us any more details."

"There isn't really any more detail. And call me Lilah, Beatrice, is it?"

I nodded, "My friends call me Betty."

She went back behind her desk and motioned us to sit down. "Betty it will be then," she smiled. Her mouth had a natural downturn that made her look as though she were perpetually distraught, but the smile lit up her face like the sun rising over the sea. Sadly, the smile quickly disappeared. "It's a simple matter of profit and loss. My Hold is small, the smallest of the ten in Glomwill. Our primary...really, our only industry is bluefin. The Arran Sea is the only place you can catch bluefin and they are considered quite a delicacy. It's not a huge industry, but it keeps my Hold profitable.

"Then, last month, the nets started to come up empty. We've run through down periods before, but never for more than a few days. Something, or someone, is taking the fish. As I said, it's not a huge industry and I have limited cash reserves on hand. I've already begun receiving buyout offers from another Hold, and if the bluefin don't come back within the month, I'll have to sell."

"When you say the nets come up empty, are you catching nothing?"

"Oh no, we still catch some fish, but not nearly enough to support our economy. We just have not been able to determine if something natural is killing the bluefin or someone else is out there fishing them out."

"How would that happen?" I asked. "Just because someone else is fishing in the same area, wouldn't there still be plenty of fish for everyone?"

"I'm afraid we don't really understand the ecology of the bluefin, Betty. We do know the numbers are limited, so we are careful not to over-fish. Our boats only go out every two or three days, and the fishing season lasts about nine months—we don't fish during spawn season or the couple of months thereafter. The money we make during the season is enough to support us the remaining months until the bluefin are back in sufficient numbers."

"It seems to me what you need is someone to study the bluefin, not hired muscle."

"We do have people working on figuring out if this is a natural problem. Maybe we have, over the years, fished them out of existence. Maybe there's some new, natural predator eating them or a disease is killing them off. What we don't have is someone to investigate the...human angle. I want you to find out if someone else is out there taking our fish."

Jewels finally piped up, "Can't you just get a tech to scry the area?"

"We've tried," Lilah sighed. "I've worked on that personally, it's just too wide an area and there's no specific target for me to be able to see properly."

I was surprised. It's unusual enough to find a troll working with humans, and now to find out she was a technician...well, trolls keep their techs close to home and they are highly valued. Something serious must have happened for her to end up here.

"OK, so you can't scry anything, but, still, if other fishing boats were out there, wouldn't some of your fisherman have seen them?"

"I don't understand it myself. This is why we appealed to Joshua, we're at our wits' end. The problem is bad enough we aren't even worrying about the ship disappearances."

"The what?" I'm not sure whether Jewels or I said it first.

"Well, some of our boats have gone out and not come home. It's sad, but it happens. Boats sink." She paused a moment. Personally, I didn't need to hear that last comment. "Our boats go out as a fleet, so if one founders, others are around to help and everyone knows what has happened. The boats go out just before dawn, but with this crisis a few captains have tried getting an early start, going out in the dark, and they've not been seen nor heard from since."

"And you don't think this is related to the absence of fish?"

"How could it be? Sailing is dangerous in the dark. A ship is lost to a shoaling reef, or a freak storm, or a mistake by the crew. None of those things would account for the fish disappearing. It's only been a small number of ships—three, I think. And other crews have done the same thing and come back without incident. I really do think it's just accidental. It's tragic, so I've issued orders banning anyone from leaving before the whole fleet sets out."

I wasn't convinced. "You can't rule out the possibilities, Lilah. But, if they are related, then finding the reason behind the disappearing fish should also reveal the reason behind the disappearing boats. Do you have any idea where we should start looking?"

"The only idea I have had is to patrol those areas. We have, over the last several days, sent small groups of boats out to do just that. Unfortunately, we haven't found anything."

"When are they patrolling?"

"During the day, once the main fishing fleet has returned. Those boats without any catch stay out and cruise around until dusk."

"No patrols at night?"

"As I said, sailing at night is dangerous and I don't want to risk more ships."

"That's where we should probably start, Betty," interrupted Jewels.

I looked at her with a raised eyebrow. "I don't like it but I think you're right." I turned back to Lilah, "I don't know enough about sailing to know what questions to ask. Where should I send the captain of my ship to ask about...charts, and stuff like that."

"My assistant is pulling charts of our main fishing grounds for you. She'll have them as you leave. If your captain wishes, I'll make available one of our more experienced fleet captains. He'll be here in my office tomorrow morning after the fleet returns. For tonight, I welcome you to stay at one of our local inns."

"Thank you, but one of the team members is an ogre, so we'll need to stay on the ship, I think." Jewels and I stood to leave.

"Nonsense! We do have a small Ogretown and I'll reserve you rooms at an inn over there. Your other companion will fit in nicely." Lilah came around her desk to meet us. "Please. Whatever you find out, let me know as soon as possible. We're getting desperate here." She clasped my hand with both her hands. I held her grip and tried to convey sympathy with my eyes and a hopeful smile, then Jewels and I turned to go.

"When we tell Sam about all this," Jewels whispered to me as we walked down the hall. "Don't forget the part about how you fell for the cat."

"I don't know what you're talking about," I muttered and quickened my pace toward the front door.

FOUR

We found Sam walking down the street looking closely at the buildings. Here and there he reached up and poked around in the exterior plaster. "Fascinating," he said as we approached. "Do you realize these walls are made of shells?"

"It's called coquina." I smirked a little at finally knowing something Sam did not.

"Fascinating," was all he said.

I hefted the package of charts Mrs. Kyle had given me. "Let's go see Captain Spanner and collect our gear. Then we can find someplace to eat."

During the time it took to get out to the ship, pass off the charts to Captain Spanner, collect our gear, register at an inn with ogre-sized rooms, and find a place to eat, we filled Sam in on the information provided by Lilah. He asked no questions until we had been seated and ordered our food. "Who is offering to buy this Hold?"

"Umm...I don't know," I conceded. "We didn't ask."

"Really?" Sam seemed surprised. "It seems to me to be quite the most important piece of information. If there is a human agency behind the loss of the bluefin, we must ask ourselves why. Are they trying to take the market away? Bluefin is, as Miss Burkah said, profitable, but not a great source of wealth. And if that were the plan, they are not dumping the fish on the Ilanerra market. I checked the day before we left; bluefin is in scant supply across the continent. It is possible they are shipping it to Gorsj or across the Straights to Durgaland, but why go to all this trouble for a mildly successful business venture? They could just as easily have presented themselves to Miss Burkah as a vendor who had sales opportunities in other markets.

"Could it be an attempt to drive the Hold out of business? If so, that begs the question of what is in this Hold to interest them. Again, they could hardly be attempting to take over a small business in such an elaborate manner. If all they are interested in is running the bluefin business, a generous offer to Miss Burkah would probably convince her to sell and seek retirement—or use her money to found a new business.

"In short, if this is a deliberate act of sabotage, the first suspect in my thinking would be the person most interested in acquiring the 'problem.' We could certainly run good Captain Spanner ragged rushing back-and-forth in the dark of night futilely seeking supposed stealthy fishermen, but it seems to me more productive to begin inquiries into the business that is seeking to add 'bluefin supplier' to its portfolio.

The sheer weight of Sam's argument pressed on my brain. "All right, Sam. You make a good case, but what do we do about it? Do we go marching into the office of this shadowy villain and say, 'Hey! Are you stealing bluefin?' I'm a man of action. Patrolling fishing holes isn't my idea of great action, but I'll take it over just trying to buttonhole a guy."

"You have not, in the past, been reluctant to give, shall we say, physical inducement to individuals to sway them to do as your employer asks. Could we not determine who the 'villain' is, then let you politely ask him to stop?"

"I've always dealt with small-timers, Sam. Somebody needs somebody to be leaned on, they hire me and I go lean on them. I can't lean on a whole corporation. Whoever this is, is big time, and he would just laugh at me. Right before he ordered someone to kill me, not to mention the two of you."

"Anybody tries to kill any of us, they get one of my spells right up their..." Jewels made a rude gesture and I turned red as I saw other diners staring at us. She carried on, "Sam's got a point, Betty. We go see this guy who's all bent on buying up little Miss Cat's business, and while you're talking, I scry him. Pick his brain a little, find out what he's up to. If he's the guy, we just turn him into Miss Cat and leave. Let her deal with him. She's probably got hired guns already on payroll and she can run a little hostile takeover of her own."

"She's not a cat, Jewels. She's a person."

"She's a troll, Betty. Don't go soft on me just 'cause she looks nice. Trolls are thugs and savages. You know it and I know it. Miss 'Lilah' might have got herself all cleaned up and running things down here and she might even know a little tech, but she's still a cat."

"Jewels," Sam jumped in to stop her. "I quite like you, but you have a list of prejudices that would fill a lengthy novel and right now they are making the people around us quite upset. Please eat your salad and do not talk." He turned to me, "Jewels's plan is surprisingly good." Jewels snorted at him around a mouthful of lettuce. "We should visit Miss Burkah's potential benefactor and let Jewels work her magic on him and see what we turn up. It could save us spending several nights out on the boat."

That clinched it. If I could avoid cruising in the boat again, so much the better.

~

In hindsight, it was stupid to go to bed that night without having Jewels set up any alarms around our rooms. But, really, what had we done? Nothing. We arrived, talked to Lilah, talked amongst ourselves. We hadn't gotten as far as actually *doing* anything. It was probably the talking at dinner. We didn't exactly try to whisper, and we hadn't set up any psychic wards, but why would we suspect the enemy was listening in?

Whoever they were, they were good. They got into each of our rooms without waking us and put us out with a spell. I went to bed that night on a soft mattress and woke up on a cold, stone floor in a dark room. As consciousness fully returned, I groaned. My arms were tied behind my back and my feet were bound together. I ached from lying who knows how long on the stone. Groans to my left told me Sam was also waking up, but I couldn't hear any sound that might be Jewels.

A bright light burst into the darkness, blinding me. I squinted hard against the light and waited for my eyes to adjust. As my vision cleared, I could see Sam's bulk, and to my right the small form of Jewels, still motionless. "What! What's going on?"

"We'll ask the questions here. First, you can tell us your names."

I immediately began counting horses in my head. I focused very hard on just counting horses.
One...two...three...

"Wise guys, eh? Look, this will be a lot easier if you just answer the questions. What are your names?"

...ten...eleven...twelve...oh look, a unicorn!...thirteen...I could hear them whispering, one loudly enough I could make out his words. "What d'you mean you can't hear 'im?...He's doing what?...I don't even know what that is. Which one's countin' horses? Alright, I'll start with him."

...twenty-seven...twenty-eight...Rough hands grabbed me and hauled me upright and to a chair. They pushed me into it and then wrapped rope around my chest to bind me to it. They tightened the rope, forcing my chest back against my arms behind me, making my shoulders scream in pain.

...forty-two...forty-three...forty-four...

"OK, you're smart enough to know we've got a 'path sittin' here tryin' to listen to your brain. So you think you can just count the little horsies and we'll get nuthin'. Well, let's see how well you can count when we're bustin' your chops."

A dark figure loomed in front of me, silhouetted by the bright light. He slapped me, not hard and using his palm, rocking my head to the side and then immediately rocked it back the other way. He kept that up for a little while, rocking my head back-and-forth several times. Then he shouted at me, "What's your name?"

...sixty-four...sixty-five...

He rocked me again. It was getting harder to focus and just count. My shoulders and neck were begging me to make it stop...sixty-nine...I ground my teeth together...seventy...

"What's your name!" No longer a question. A demand.

"Betty! His name's Betty Sterling." A new voice, further away behind the light.

I uttered a mental curse I knew the telepath would "hear," and focused on counting. I picked cows this time. Purple cows...one...two...three...

"Good. Now we're gettin' somewhere." My tormenter sighed and pulled a chair up for himself. He sat in front of me and leaned in close enough that I could see his face. He actually had a nice face, sympathetic even. No! I have to focus on the cows... four...five...

"Betty? Nice name for a girly-boy like you." I promptly head-butted him, which earned me an even harder slap for my trouble.

"That's enough of that, 'Betty.'" He twisted my name into a vulgarity.

Fourteen! I was mentally shouting now... fifteen!...sixteen! The questioner pushed my head around some more, timing his words to the rocking of my head. "See (push) we want (push) to know (push) why (a little harder push) you're askin' (push) questions (push) about (push) fish."

...thirty...thirty-one...I deliberately looked away from his face, turning my eyes downward and I saw the

tip of a wand tucked into his belt. It wasn't sheathed. I
suddenly had a new idea.

"We're working for the Alpha Warlord of
Durgaland. He sent us to find out why he's running out
of tuna. He likes to eat it raw, you know." I put all my
attention on thinking about my story, even conjuring
up an image of a generic troll all decked out in battle
armor. I don't know if trolls wear battle armor, but
probably neither do these guys.

"Ah, now you're just gettin' cute," said the
questioner. He rocked me a few more times. "Why are
you askin' questions about the fish?"

"I'm telling you," I was breathless from the pain
and had to focus hard on keeping my thoughts in line
with what I was saying. "His High Mightiness wants
tuna, and I'm not going to say no to him. Nobody says
no to His High Mightiness and lives."

More pushing. He leaned in closer and his face
didn't look quite so sympathetic. "Why are you askin'
questions about the fish!"

"Between you and me, I don't even like tuna. And I
never eat anything raw. Do you? But trolls have funny
tastes."

He grunted and decided to change up his tactics. He
gave me a couple of quick jabs using his knuckles to my
lower abdomen. "Why are you askin' questions about
the fish!"

I could see the tip of his wand starting to glow and
it was everything I could do to not let my thoughts
stray from the image of a troll in battle armor. This
bozo probably never encountered any serious
resistance and was already getting mad. Too mad.

"Frankly," I grunted around the pain in my belly, "I don't like to eat fish at all. Swimming around in the ocean, drinking fish piss. It's disgusting, man. But I gotta do what the Warlord wants."

The guy rabbit-punched me again. His eyes were widening and spittle formed on his lips as he shouted at me, "Why are you askin' about the fish!"

"You know, your breath smells like the Warlord's breath. I figured there wasn't anybody in the world that ate fish raw, and here you are stinking the place up with that smell. There's no tuna that's worth smelling that."

"I didn't ask you about my personal hygiene." His voice dropped to a menacing purr as he jabbed me again. "Tell me why you're askin' about the fish!"

"Oh, come on! Back off a little and let me breathe clean air. I can't think with that rotten fish smell in my..." That's when it happened. The guy had gotten so mad he started thinking about wanting to kill me. And the wand in his pocket obliged. The telepath sitting in the back had just enough time to yell, "Gus! Calm ..." and the wand exploded. I tucked my head down to my chest and pulled up my knees and the force of the discharge blew me backwards and onto my back. I had just enough time to think, "Hmm, ice wand," before I blacked out.

FIVE

"Come on, Betty, wake up." Someone was rubbing my arms and shoulders. I was cold, very cold and I began shivering as I woke up. It took a moment for my brain to catch back up to now and I opened my eyes. Sam was still massaging warmth back into my upper body. I groaned, rolled over and tried to push up. Sam helped me sit up, and left me there, slouched over and taking deep breaths.

I looked around the room. The bright light had been coming from a lantern, which was now lying on the floor beside a table where it had sat and been shone directly at me. Behind the table slumped a figure I assumed to be the telepath. Nearby, the frozen torso of my questioner lay at a grotesque angle. A little further away was his lower body; the ice spell had frozen him and then cracked him in two. Near his legs, Sam had crawled over and was tending to Jewels, who seemed to be waking up.

I put my hands to my face and rubbed my numbed cheeks. Ice crystals fell from my beard and I vigorously rubbed my head to get more out of my hair.

"That was a brilliant maneuver, Betty," Sam said as he helped Jewels up. "However, it was completely unnecessary and quite dangerous. Had it been a fire or lightning wand rather than ice, you probably would have been killed by the blast. And, while you were playing with our interrogators, I had rolled off to the side and worked free of my bonds. Another moment and I would have been able to take care of both of them without resorting to random wand explosions. As it was, in the confusion I rendered the telepath unconscious."

"Thanks, Sam, but how would I know what you're doing? I'm not a telepath. And the wand wouldn't have hit me full blast because it was halfway down his pants. I admit," I picked some ice out of my ear, "it got me enough. By the way, what were you thinking that made them pick on me?"

"When I need to disguise my thoughts, I begin humming all the major and minor scales, but, I randomly intermix them. Any telepath trying to listen to my thoughts hears only a cacophony, nothing coherent."

Sam picked Jewels up and she buried her face in his neck. He stood, stooped over because the ceiling wasn't high enough for him. I pushed myself to my feet and went to the lantern. "What do we do with this guy?" I asked Sam, pointing at the telepath.

Sam considered for a moment. "Leave him," he finally answered. "We know he is a tech and so we cannot let him wake, but Jewels is not in a condition to keep him out and I would rather not have to club him over and over."

"But," I objected, "he represents information, served up on a platter. Shouldn't we try to question him?"

"Without our gear and with Jewels still somewhat incapacitated, do you really want to match wits with a telepath? And who knows what other spells he knows! Come on, Betty. We know whatever is going on here is big, and the person behind it is ruthless. Let us retreat for now, and regroup. Then we can begin our investigations."

I turned, looking around at the rough-hewn walls and began taking in our surroundings for the first time. We stood in the middle of a small cavern with rock walls, floor, and ceiling. There was a faint dampness and as I realized we were underground, I began to feel the pressure above me. I like to think I'm not afraid of anything, but right then I began to realize I was afraid of being buried alive underground. I didn't like the feeling at all.

"OK, let's just get out of here." I hoped Sam couldn't hear the fear in my voice. "Which way do we go?"

"I presume through that opening right over there," Sam nodded toward a dark patch in the wall. "And then we just take whatever tunnels are moving up."

"Up is good. Let's get out of here." I grabbed the lamp and we started moving, slowly. I was still recovering from the ice blast and Sam was almost crawling, walking both crouched and stooped over, because the ceiling of the mine had only been built for humans. "Here," I offered, "let me carry Jewels. It'll make it easier for you to move."

"Guys," her little voice was muffled by Sam's neck. "I can walk. Just put me down, Sam." Sam put Jewels down and then crouched, adopting an ape-like stance with his hands on the ground. Jewels stood still for a moment, eyes closed and taking deep, slow breaths. After a moment, she opened her eyes and her body seemed to briefly ripple, as though muscles were flexing in waves from her feet to her head. She took another deep breath and then set off, faster than her legs should be able to move. Sam and I struggled to keep up.

The oppressive weight of the ground above me was compounded by the darkness pressing in around the globe of light coming from the lamp. Jewels moved confidently, taking turns without hesitation whenever other tunnels forked away. The only sound was of our boots hitting the rock and ragged panting, especially from Sam and myself. I felt only half thawed out and Sam was almost crawling, moving forward with his hands and his feet, but keeping his knees off the hard rock. He looked like some sort of huge, ungainly bear slouching its way out of its winter den.

The thought made me chuckle. Sam was less bear and more a child's stuffed doll. Jewels looked back harshly, "What's funny? Keep up!" And then she was off, and I had to focus on walking. Several hours later by my internal clock—but what was actually probably less than half an hour—we rounded a turn and could see lighter black in front of us. I quickened my pace and had almost caught up with Jewels by the time we emerged from the tunnel.

Sam groaned and collapsed on the ground, stretching his arms over his head and pointing his toes as he worked out the kinks in his muscles. The area around the mouth of the tunnel was a clearing carved into the side of a hill. Behind us, rolling hills led up to spired mountains trying to touch the sky. Plain block buildings were scattered around the clearing, but there appeared to be no signs of occupation. Jewels soon confirmed it.

"I can't 'hear' anyone nearby. Unless anyone's out there wearing a shield while they sleep, I think we're safe."

I shuttered the lantern and set it down. Sam got himself upright and stretched some more, all while looking around. "I believe this must be a tapped-out mine," he said. "I noticed as we ascended the tunnel system that we were moving in a large spiral, designed to create a gradual slope for carts to be brought up. Also, obviously, the tunnel we were in was not natural. Those buildings would be the miners' quarters, but the lack of people and equipment indicates no one is working this site."

"That's all fine and good," I said. "But where are we?" We all walked toward the edge of the clearing and looked down over the hillside. To the east, the sky was turning orange as the sun rose and far below we could make out the ocean. Along the edge of the sea a dark, irregular smudge indicated a town. "If that's Darfa, we weren't taken far."

"It's too far away for me to hear anyone down there, so we might as well start walking." Jewels followed her own advice and began picking her way down a path that switch-backed its way down to the shore plain. Sam and I both heaved sighs and started after her.

We trudged on for some time as the day grew brighter. When we reached the bottom of the hill the road straightened out and ran toward the town. We trundled on, and soon came to an intersection where a large road running parallel to the sea crossed our small lane. Here we saw our first signs of life as large floaters and carts passed by, taking passengers or cargo to their destinations.

"Wait a minute," Jewels halted. Her eyes went distant. After a moment, she shook herself. "That was Miss Cat; wow, has she got range! It wasn't much more than a whisper, but we could hear each other and she's sending a floater for us. We might as well wait." Jewels plopped down in the grass, and Sam and I followed suit.

I watched the traffic float past. Very little came from the direction of the town, which must be Darfa if Lilah could establish telepathic contact with Jewels. What did come from town immediately turned onto the larger road. No one was interested in heading up into the hills from where we came.

I let my mind wander. Whatever was going on here wasn't just about fish. You don't kidnap and interrogate people over fish. And, the funny thing was, I was happy about that. I had felt out-of-place and unneeded ever since Mr. Cristof sent me out on this expedition. I'm not a detective, I'm an enforcer. And if the other side employed guys like Gus and that telepath, then an enforcer was exactly what was needed. Now that we had a target, I felt like I could make an actual contribution. All that remained was to determine whom, exactly, that target was.

A floater approached from the town and crossed the intersection to us. It was a plain, wooden platform with a rug crudely tacked on to it. I agreed with Jewels when she snorted, "They sent a flying carpet to pick us up?"

The operator stared at her with a hard glint in his eye. "'Twas all that was available on short notice that would carry all three of ya, with one of ya bein' an ogre. 'Course, ye could always walk inter town."

"No thanks," Jewels put obviously fake sweetness into her voice and then levitated up to the floater. Sam and I climbed aboard, and the operator turned the floater and sped back to Darfa. In an uncovered floater there was no opportunity for talk, and we traveled in silence until we reached the Hold office. Lilah was standing in the doorway to meet us.

"Thank goodness you are all alright! I've been scrying the area ever since the inn reported your rooms were empty and I had about given up hope of finding you." She came forward and I thought she might hug me, but changed her mind at the last minute and just took my hand. I felt a twinge of disappointment.

I got gruff to cover my emotion. "We're not going to talk here. Or anywhere near here. Miss Burkah—Lilah—would you mind accompanying us out to our ship?" I didn't pause to wait for an answer. "Thank you. The faster we get on board, the safer I'll feel." The driver of the floater looked like he might object, but thought better of it as I herded Lilah toward the harbor.

"I will go and get our gear from the inn," Sam

offered.

"Leave it," I told him. "We can come back later, but they might still be watching it."

"Who's they?" asked Lilah.

"On the ship!" I pointed and placed my hand on her back to gently prod her along. I didn't take the hand away.

~

"That's...that's just unbelievable!"

We were on board *Sea Lily*, our hired ship, and had put out far enough from port that even Lilah said she couldn't hear anyone. Safe, I hoped, from mental eavesdropping, we covered the highlights of our overnight adventures. Lilah remained silent, for the most part, only uttering slight interjections at the more violent parts of the tale, until we reached the end of the story and she said it was unbelievable.

We all just looked at her. "It's not that I don't believe you. I do. Those mines in the hills are part of Taylor Harris's Hold. They're gold miners and quite rich. In fact, it's Taylor that's offered to buy me out. But I just can't believe he would have anything to do with this. He's always been very friendly and...why does he want a fishing operation? He runs gold mines. Gold!" She said it with a kind of finality.

"I wondered why my head felt fuzzy," said Jewels. "They may not be working that mine anymore, but there's still gold in there. Not much, but enough to make me feel like magic would be too much effort."

"It didn't stop you from enhancing," I retorted.

"If I hadn't we'd still be down there trying to find our way out!"

"Children," Sam clucked at us. "Of more immediate worry is why this Mr. Harris would be attempting to run Ms. Burkah out of business."

"He can't be behind this!"

"I understand your reluctance to implicate him, Ms. Burkah. But he is the most obvious culprit at this time."

"Then it's simple." Finally something I knew how to do. "We need to go ask him. I doubt he would let us just walk in and chat, so it's an assault. We'll need whatever information you can give us on his Hold, his Hold office, and where he lives. We'll go back in to shore and meet in Sam's room at the inn. Jewels can ward it, we can get our gear, and you can give us everything you have on the miners. Then we move out. I still owe them for Gus."

SIX

At the inn, I began pulling stuff out of my bag. The gold-weaved mail had cost me a lot. For over a year I lived on beans and rice, with the occasional bowl of rice and beans for variety. It was more than worth it. The mail would protect me against conventional weapons and the fine gold threads would shield me against techs. The hood was also gold-weaved and would block my thoughts completely. I had two wands, one fire and one nature, both in gold-plated sheaths. I chuckled. If Gus had his wand sheathed in gold, I wouldn't have been able to provoke him into accidentally setting it off.

Jewels had finished establishing wards around the room and glared at me petulantly. "I hate it when you wear that stuff anywhere near me, Betty. The gold makes me feel stuffy and I can't hear you at all. It's like you're not even there!"

"It has the same effect on enemy techs, Jewels. That's why I wear it."

"Ick," she said as she wrapped her arms around herself. "I could just shield you, you know."

"Thanks, Jewels, but you won't always be right beside me. And I want your mind clear to focus on your own spells without worrying what's being tossed at me."

"Well, take it over there," she pointed to the far corner, "so I won't have to feel it."

I obliged, dragging my gear over to the other side of the room and going through it to make sure I had everything. A knock at the door set us all on alert.

"It's me. Lilah."

I pulled my fire wand and opened the door slightly. She wasn't alone. "This is the captain of my police force, David Graisson. He's all right."

I pulled back the door to let them in. Graisson offered his left hand to shake. His right arm was missing. "Aye, lost it in a boating accident years ago." He answered my stare. "'Tis what grounded me. Now I spends me time fishing for criminals." He grinned at me through his grizzled whiskers.

Lilah moved to the bed and spread out a map. "We're here," she said pointing to a dot on the west coast of the Sea of Arran. She traced a line around a series of marked towns on the coast. "This is my Hold. To the north is Dylan Murphrie's Hold. He's a trader. This area here," she outlined the hills lying west of her Hold, "is Taylor's Hold. He's got gold mines running all through the hills and mountains. Most of the active ones are deeper inland. His Director's Office is currently in Bluth, here." She stabbed down at a sizable mark west and a little north of Darfa.

"That's where we'll go then. Can we take this map with us?"

"I've prepared a tell-disc with a detailed imprint of the map and all the information David could give me."

Lilah held out a small, thin metal disc, telepathically imprinted with her thoughts. Jewels jumped in and snatched it.

"Let me have that. Betty wouldn't be able to see it anyway, through all his 'special' armor."

Lilah looked at me with a quizzical lift to her eyebrows, but I just shrugged it away. "Jewels can see those discs better and faster than I can anyway. Just so we're clear, though, can you tell us what you put on that disc, Captain Graisson?"

"Aye. Ye'll not want to be travelin' by night through the hills, so if it be your thinkin' to sneak in, ye'll have to stay off the beaten track. I've chased a few thieves into those crags, and I've laid out a more friendly path on Miss Lilah's map on that disc. It will take ye to the south and ye'll come into town that way, by which way ye'll be less likely to be noticed as well as have easier travelin'. At night, when ye set up camp, be sure ye keep watch, as thieves use tapped-out mines for hidey-holes and stashin' of loot and the like."

"Thank you, Captain Graisson. Anything else?"

"I've been fishin' since I was knee high to a fairy, lad. When ye be settin' out to make a catch, ye best be fishin' in the right place usin' the right bait."

"Bait? We don't have any bait..."

"Then ye be needin' to find some, don't ye, lad?"

~

We thanked Lilah and Captain Graisson and saw them out, then set about planning our approach. Jewels took the tell-disc and focused on it, letting its imprinted images fill her mind. Sam and I discussed Captain Graisson's advice.

"What did he mean by bait? And what bait would we have?"

Sam was lost in thought for a moment. "It just may be that we, ourselves, are the bait. We need information, correct?" I nodded for him to continue. "Let us assume this Hold Director, Mr. Harris, is our enemy. He has thus already shown an interest in our activities and shown himself to be ruthless in prosecuting his endeavors toward his primary objective. He wants information from us, and we want information from him. A trade, therefore, would seem to be in order."

"You mean sell out Lilah? Not on your..."

"Hear me out, Betty. We need Mr. Harris to think about his plans so Jewels can read his thoughts. But, we cannot be obvious in doing so. We conceal Jewels and me, and you enter Bluth alone. When accosted, you proffer your services as though you have determined to betray your allies here on the coast. When taken to Mr. Harris, you encourage him to talk about the overall plan. Jewels and I will be nearby. Jewels will read his thoughts, get all the information we need and then we break in and extract you."

"I don't like it, Sam. If we're going to do it that way, you should be the one to go in. You're better at faking things like that. Also, it will be easier for me to sneak around with Jewels than you. But, don't you think he'll have wards around the place? And armed guards?"

"That may be the case," Sam sighed. "And, I agree I am better at dissembling than you. I do not know of a better way to approach this Mr. Harris. Perhaps one will present itself when we reach Bluth." He looked over at our elven companion. "Are you ready, Jewels?"

"Just a minute, guys. I want to make sure I've got everything down correctly. I'll give Miss Cat one thing, she knows how to do an imprint."

I sighed. "Let's get some sleep and we'll set out tomorrow morning. Jewels, I need to talk to Captain Spanner, so could you drop the mental wards?" I called Spanner on a tell and informed him we would be gone for several days. He thanked me and told me he and his crew would take the opportunity to explore the Arran Sea using the charts we had given him earlier. "I might need to come back here someday, and a seaman always likes to know the waters before he carries passengers into them," he told me. I didn't think we would need his services any time soon, so I wished him luck in his explorations.

There was a chill in the air the next morning, and a dense fog had settled in overnight. We set out early and I was glad for the extra padding under my mail. Jewels made it a point to walk several lengths in front of me, which was probably just as well, since she had a clearer picture of Lilah's tell-disc map and Graisson's route. Despite the early hour, the town was bustling with activity. Fishermen obviously are used to rising before the sun and were about their business for the day, and shops and other businesses were already open for them.

Lilah provided a floater, a nice enclosed-cab model this time, not a flying carpet, to take us to the edge of the foothills. We would have to make the rest of the journey on foot. Loaded down as I was with mail and a backpack with camping gear, I was grateful for a brief reprieve.

We followed Graisson's route through the hill country without much trouble. Jewels "heard" small groups of bandits, but only one was brave enough to challenge us. On the second day, a group of six men came charging out of the rocks in the early morning while we were breaking camp. They weren't shielded and Jewels knew they were coming, so they never even got close enough to try and damage us with their rusty knives and swords.

I had both wands ready when they came and used the nature wand to carve a ditch right in front of them, and as they tripped and fell, I used the fire wand to explode fireballs on the ground in their midst. One slightly more intelligent guy hung back and actually pulled a wand and fired it at me. Lucky for me, he aimed it right at me rather than at the ground nearby, so the gold weave caused the spell to sputter and die without doing any harm. The one shot was all he got off before Sam reached him and knocked him out with his staff.

"Let him go, now," I said to Jewels. She had been levitating one bandit around our camp and dropped him from about ten lengths. We packed up our things and set out, leaving the survivors to clean up the mess.

We arrived at Bluth late in the afternoon of the fourth day out from Darfa. The southern approach was through a series of rocky gullies, which kept us hidden. As we neared the town, Jewels became increasingly agitated.

"I can't hear anyone," she whined. "This close I should feel the presence of thoughts even if I weren't trying to listen, but it's like a ghost town. Not even a whisper."

"They could all be down in mines, surrounded by gold," Sam suggested.

I chimed in with, "Or they all wear shields."

"It's just really weird to be this close to a place with lots of people and not be able to even sense any thoughts. I'm worried, guys."

We reached the end of a gully and clambered up through some rocks until we could peek over a hill and see the town spread out below us.

"All right, now I'm downright scared," Jewels hissed.

The town below had an impermanent look, with hastily thrown-together wood buildings. The miners probably moved their town wholesale whenever new mines opened, but it made the whole place look as if it were ready to fall apart. There were no roads, as such, just paths meandering between the shacks. A primary road entered the town from off to the east and a few transport floaters were moving in and out of town.

Throughout the town, figures shambled through the streets. Full cargo floats were being dragged to storage buildings, while empty ones were being taken north, where we assumed the mines were located. I looked at Jewels; her eyes were wide and she was chewing on a fingernail.

"I don't get it," she said. "I still can't hear anything!"

Sam pulled a telescope from his backpack and began scanning the town below. "There is definitely something strange about the people," he muttered.

"They seem quite listless for mine workers. And I do not see anyone going into or coming out of any of the buildings that appear to be shops or taverns. I only see traffic to and from the mines...ah, there is the Hold Office sigil. It is on the larger building to the east side of town."

"Do we follow through with our original plan?" I asked. During the trek to Bluth we had haggled over who would go in and how we would arrange to hide nearby, but with no clue what the town looked like, we were just tossing out guesses.

"I think, rather, a nighttime reconnoiter would be better," Sam opined. "Let us pull back and sleep a few hours until the second watch, and then go explore the Hold office. I want some answers before we make any moves."

Jewels and I weren't arguing the point and we slid back into the gully and made a cold camp. We got what snatches of sleep we could muster, but we were all too keyed up to really get any rest. We waited well into the night, then suited up and climbed back up out of the gully.

Anthelles, the first moon, was high in the sky when we started picking our way down into Bluth. The second moon, Zerion, was just beginning to rise above the eastern peaks. The strong moonlight made it harder to keep to shadows, but we managed, sliding from rock formation to clumps of brush to more rocks. After a half-hour of crawling and creeping downhill, we reached the outskirts of the closest buildings.

"Let's take a minute to catch our breath," I whispered. I went ahead and pulled out my wands and leaned against the wall of a shack. Jewels plopped down in the dirt and Sam crouched down and lowered his head, taking deep, steady breaths. "All right," I commanded after a moment, "let's move around to the side. Sam, have you got the location of the Hold Office in your head?"

Sam nodded and we crept off to the right. We took it slow, but we saw no movement, heard no sounds, and saw no lights in any window. Jewels kept shaking her head, her way of saying she still could not detect any thoughts. The town felt dead, despite all the people we had seen earlier.

We reached the Hold Office, and I carefully tried the door. The door was locked, but Sam pulled a kit out of a pocket and went to work on the lock. Within a few minutes he had it unlocked and opened the door with a slight creak. I paused and listened, but heard no movement or cry. The door was large enough for Sam to fit through and the inside was spacious. It quickly became apparent the building, despite its size, was single-story and therefore plenty roomy enough for an ogre. The main room we were in had doors branching out on three sides. I looked at Jewels, but she just shrugged her shoulders.

The door to the right led into a hallway lined with more doors, all locked. I assumed these were offices, but I wasn't ready to break into any of them. Returning to the main room, we went through the door opposite the main entrance, but this just led to a conference room with a large table and a dozen or more chairs scattered around.

Our last choice was the door off to the left of the

main room. We found ourselves in a small hall that almost immediately turned right. There was a locked door on the left, and then another door at the end of the hall just past the turn. That door was unlocked so I peeked in and saw what looked like a sitting room. We crept in and went to another door across the room. That led into a bedroom and that's where we found Taylor Harris.

He was dead.

SEVEN

We stood staring at the corpse lying on the bed. Despite his lack of vitality, he didn't look bad, just cold...and stiff. Jewels confirmed it was Harris, based on an image included on Lilah's tell-disc.

I finally broke the silence. "He can't have been dead long. He hasn't even started to decay."

"Something stinks about this, Betty."

"He's dead, Jewels. Dead people stink."

"Not him! This!" Jewels struggled to find the right words. "There are people running around the town, but I can't hear them. This guy's just lying dead on his bed, instead of in a death hall like normal people. And the town is dead at night, no lights, no taverns, no nothing. It stinks."

"I have to agree with Jewels," Sam said. "There is something terribly wrong about this situation. We need to see whether we can find any records anywhere in this Hold House. And then we need to get out of here and get back to Darfa."

It was as we were leaving the bedroom that we heard the front door squeak. I readied my wands and I saw Sam grip his staff more tightly. I turned toward Jewels just as she screamed. The dead body of Taylor

Harris was up and had wrapped its arms around Jewels and was squeezing. Jewels drew in a deep breath and exploded. Her self-centered fireball blew Sam and me away, singeing me and setting Harris's body on fire. Despite the damage, the body didn't make a sound or react in any way. Jewels was still screaming and had resorted to wiggling and kicking, trying to free herself from its grip.

Sam stumbled to his feet and rushed toward the flaming figure and swung his staff down between Jewels's head and Harris's body. The wood hit the burning flesh of the corpse with a dull thud and one of the arms fell out of his body and hit the floor in a shower of sparks. Jewels dropped to the floor and fell to her hands and knees, crying and retching. Sam swung again, a giant roundhouse that hit the corpse in its chest and sent it flying backwards into a wall. I turned my nature wand on the floor beneath the corpse as it struggled to rise and the wood and dirt below it dissolved and the body fell into a deep hole.

I turned back to the doorway leading to the hall, where I could hear shuffling footsteps coming closer. "Sam. Jewels. We've got company."

They pushed through the door, corpses every one, just like Harris. They shuffled in toward us without sound, arms reaching up to grab us. Sam whirled his staff, striking the first couple of bodies and knocking them back into those behind. "Betty! We can't fight off this many, and Jewels still can't concentrate!"

"Out the back door, folks!" I yelled. I aimed a fireball at the floor in front of the corpses, delaying them briefly as the front ranks began to burn. Then I turned and ran back into the bedroom, using the nature wand to carve a seam down the wood of the opposite wall. I hit the wall with my shoulder, crashing out into the street. Sam pushed through after me, carrying Jewels in one arm.

There were throngs of animated corpses in the streets. They did not seem to be immediately aware of our presence, but soon turned toward us like dogs tracking a scent. I described an arc to the left using the nature wand to open up a ditch, but my emotions were running a little strong and the gap that appeared was wider and deeper than I had intended and the ground rumbled and shook with the movement.

I grabbed Sam's arm and pulled him to the right, using the fire wand to blast corpses back from our path. Sam set Jewels down and she pulled herself upright with her eyes blazing. Levitating up to the same height as Sam, Jewels focused and pointed, shooting out streams of freezing cold, hitting the corpses and icing them in place. Sam kept his staff whirling, hitting the frozen corpses and shattering them. Between the three of us, we forced open a hole toward the eastern mountains and ran.

"Where are we going?" Sam grunted.

"We get away from these things and then circle back to the south, get our supplies and run back to Darfa as fast as we can."

"Can we keep up this pace?" Sam asked. "Those things are not going to rest as we must."

"Who knows how long they'll keep up the chase. But we can't fight something that doesn't feel pain and doesn't stop coming."

The trip back toward Darfa was a blur of exhaustion. Sam and I took turns carrying Jewels while she tried to sleep. When we couldn't keep going, we would drop to the ground and sleep while Jewels kept watch. When the monsters got close, she would wake us and our plodding run would begin again.

We dumped supplies other than food to keep the weight down, and we ate cold rations while we trudged on. Sam and I tried to talk at first to distract us from the drudgery of moving forward, trying to stay ahead of the creatures. But Jewels quickly asked us to keep quiet so she could sleep, which I thought was unfair. If she could sleep while cradled in my or Sam's arms, she could certainly ignore a little conversation.

After the first couple of sleep-run cycles, it didn't matter. I doubted Sam could keep a coherent sentence together and I knew I couldn't. My eyes were heavy and I started tripping over rocks because I wasn't lifting my feet anymore, just shuffling them along the ground. Once I went down while carrying Jewels and barely managed to twist so my shoulder hit the ground first instead of falling on top of her.

That was the end of that cycle, as I couldn't drag myself up again. I was beginning to hallucinate by the time we reached level ground at last. Sam and I both fell heavily to the ground. I rolled over and looked at Jewels. "How long has it been?"

"A day and a half, maybe?" She answered. "We covered ground a lot faster coming than we did going."

"Any chance you can reach Lilah from here?"

"I don't see how," she replied. "We're still way too far from Darfa for me to hear anyone." She turned and climbed back up the trail to watch for the monsters.

I had long since stopped wearing my hood, as I was sweating far too much to make it comfortable and I really didn't care who could hear my thoughts. There wasn't much for them to hear other than "put one foot in front of the other." I rolled onto my back, and, as I drifted off to sleep, I thought, "Mr. Cristof, what have you gotten me into?"

For the first time since the chase began, I dreamed. In my dream I was in Cristof's office, sitting at the same table where he had first hired me. "What's the problem, Betty?" he asked me. I proceeded to tell him, at length, about our troubles, concentrating on the monsters chasing us through the mountains. "I'll take care of them, Betty. Just get yourselves back to Darfa."

"Betty! Wake up, Betty..." I squinted my eyes open to see Jewels sitting beside me, shaking me. I grunted and rolled over, pushing myself up. "It's been hours," Jewels said. "I let you and Sam sleep, but those things must have finally given up."

I chuckled. "Maybe Cristof chased 'em away."

"What?" Jewels looked at me like I was crazy.

"Nothing. Just a dream I had. They're probably just afraid to come down out of the rocks."

"Whatever the reason," Sam interjected, "we have had a decent rest and we should set out as quickly as possible..."

Sam was interrupted by the sight of a floater speeding toward us. We stood watching it until we saw it was the same floater and driver that had brought us out here several days ago.

"Ahoy!" he sang out. "We've had people out scrying

for you for the past couple o' days. Sorry it took me so long to get out here. Hop on in, you folks look spent."

~

Lilah absorbed our tale in silence, brooding with her head resting on her fists. We were back aboard *Sea Lily*. Captain Spanner had pulled into port only hours before we returned. Lilah had not even protested going aboard—her scryers may have picked up some of what had transpired. When we finished, she had only one word.

"Draug."

"What?"

She heaved a huge sigh. "I know only the stories. Stories I thought, before tonight, were just tales to scare children. Among the Durgah," she used the Troll's name for themselves, "there are stories of powerful trollmen—what you call 'technicians'—who could possess the dead, manipulating them as a puppeteer manipulates his puppets." She hugged herself. "I thought they were just stories," she repeated.

"So...we're dealing with a troll technician?" I asked.

"Great," Jewels said under her breath, "more cats."

Lilah's eyes hardened. I looked at Jewels and said, "Can you just stop that?" I turned back to Lilah, "Can you tell us more about the...what did you call them?"

"Draug," she answered. "I do not know if a trollman would be the only one who could raise draugur, but the tales come from my people. In the legends, a draug is merely a lifeless body controlled by the trollman who possesses it. The trollman can see through the body's eyes and hear through its ears, but cannot make the body speak. A draug is a silent worker who does not tire, nor eat, nor feel pain."

"That sounds exactly like what we encountered in Bluth," Sam added. "Those walking corpses did not make a sound, nor feel any pain, and they did not stop coming until we dismembered them."

Lilah shuddered. "I can't imagine any Durgah willing to do such a thing. Though we tell children stories of draugur, they are meant only as scary tales for the thrill of feeling fright. All the trollmen in the tales are evil, and hearing your story I believe only someone truly evil would do such a thing."

"So it's off to Durgaland," I sighed.

"No," said Lilah. "The trollman must be nearby. He had to be there in Bluth when you were there."

"Here is what we know." Sam began ticking items off on his fingers. "First, someone is attempting to put Ms. Burkah out of business by shutting of the supply of bluefin in the Sea of Arran. Second, we assume this same someone has killed Mr. Harris and his workers and is using them as draug to continue working the gold mines.

"So, we must determine what these two campaigns have in common. The takeover of Mr. Harris's mining operation is obvious—to control the supply of gold. How does Ms. Burkah's operation fit in with Mr. Harris's? My first assumption is someone is attempting to take over all ten Holds in Glomwill Holdings. Ms. Burkah, what businesses are the other Holds involved in?"

Lilah sat and thought. "Dylan Murphrie is involved in trade. He has a major seaport northeast of here and trades with Gorsj and Durgaland and even sends ships far to the west to The Islands and Llarashome. Brian Lanfer is a cattle farmer. Tarik Milner and Joria Wenshom are both financiers, they deal strictly in monetary investments. Borik Drelver is a construction magnate—he builds corporate and public buildings all over Ilanerra and Gorsj. Prizm oversees an elf enclave that manufactures a lot of our equipment. Bertie Monclear is a shipbuilder and Hugh Glomwill runs the Tube for all of Ilanerra—his grandfather built the first Tube stations and it is how he gathered all these other businesses together into one conglomerate."

Jewels whistled. "If someone took over all ten Holds, they would be rolling in most of the money in Berrea!"

Lilah smiled, brightening her face. "Not quite the whole world, Jewels, but, yes, a large part of the economy of Ilanerra and a good deal of business from Gorsj and Durgaland would run through that person's hands."

"I think," Sam began, "we should consider the possibility the person or persons behind these occurrences is also operating in the other Holds. At the very least, we can contact the other Hold Directors and ask them if anything unusual is happening."

"That should be our next step," Lilah agreed. "What happened in Taylor's Hold concerns all of the Hold Directors, and it needs to be reported. I think it's time to call a Directors Meeting and I can host it here."

I sighed. "As much as I hated fighting those draug, I think I'd rather do that than sit in a bunch of meetings."

Eight

It took a couple of days to arrange the Directors Meeting. Two days of sitting around without much to do. I wanted to let Lilah handle everything in the meeting, but she insisted all three of us must be in attendance as eyewitnesses to the happenings in Bluth. After some haggling via tell-relay stations with the other eight Directors, it was decided to hold the meeting in Braysport, Dylan Murphrie's trade center north of Darfa. There was a Tube hub station there and the other Directors would all travel there first anyway.

While Lilah was still working on the meeting plans, an unexpected visitor arrived. Sam, Jewels, and I were sitting outside Lilah's office when a small floater stopped in front of us and Joshua Cristof emerged. Sam and Jewels, having never met him, barely glanced in his direction, but I hopped up and greeted him.

"Mr. Cristof!" I shook his hand. "What brings you here?" I was vaguely worried he might be here to fire us for taking so long on what should have been a simple expedition.

"Just checking up on the job, Mr. Sterling. I like to get first-hand reports from my field agents." He smiled, and I felt my worry fade away.

"Is this the guy who hired you, Betty?" Jewels sounded a bit suspicious.

"Indeed, I am Joshua Cristof, Miss...?"

"Jewels. No 'Miss.' Just Jewels."

"I am pleased to meet you, Jewels." Cristof, rather than bend over to take her hand as most people do when greeting an elf, actually squatted down to put himself almost at eye-level. It was a gesture of respect elves almost never get, and Jewels' eyes widened in surprise. I had a brief pang thinking that I never did that myself for any elf, not even Jewels.

Jewels reached out to take Cristof's hand. "Thank you. Pleased to meet you, too." Then Jewels glanced up at me with a hint of worry in her eyes. "I think you should get that report from Betty right away."

"Yes, I think we should fill you in," Sam said, rising from where he had been sitting cross-legged on the sidewalk. "I'm Samhradh Jrorgh." He extended his hand to Cristof.

Cristof surprised me again; he greeted Sam with a traditional ogre bow, clasping his hands in front of his chest and saying something in Ogrish I couldn't understand.

Sam returned the bow and replied in Ogrish. He then turned to me with a mischievous smile, "You should learn to do this, Betty."

I was getting annoyed. Cristof was making me feel inadequate in front of my own friends. "I can practice later," I grumped. "Let's find a private place to talk."

"The inn?" Sam asked. "The rooms are large enough, and Jewels can make sure we are not overheard."

"An excellent suggestion!" Cristof enthused. "Lead the way, Mr. Sterling." He fell into step next to me as we made our way down the street. "And how have you been doing?"

"I'm afraid we're not making much progress. Every time we follow up on a lead, the situation gets... murkier."

Cristof waved my concerns away with his hand. "You can give me details of the project when we're secure. What I want to know is how you, personally, are handling these situations."

I pondered his question as we walked. "I prefer acting to talking, but...so far, what action there has been, has kind of been desperate, and then we spend a lot of time talking before ending up in another desperate situation. I feel like a fish out of water." Cristof and Sam both chuckled, while Jewels laughed out loud. "What? What did I say?"

"*Fish out* of water?" Jewels emphasized the words.

"Oh," I was a little embarrassed over my accidental pun. I talked faster to cover the slip, "It's just...I feel lost. I'm just blundering around, with no idea what the problem really is or what I can do to fix it."

Cristof clapped me on the back. "Well, then, it's good for you I came by. I specialize in helping lost people," and he gave me a big grin.

Once we were in Sam's room and warded, we laid out the progress of the mission to Cristof. He listened without interruption and continued thinking in silence once we were finished. "I certainly don't disagree with Miss Burkah calling the Directors Meeting," he finally offered. "However, the correct action plan, since you are a man of action, would be to find the Durgah technician—what did you say Miss Burkah called him? A trollman, yes—behind the deaths and re-animation of the people in Bluth."

"How would we do that?" I asked.

"I think Miss Burkah should be able to provide some insight there. After all, she's the one who is familiar with the legends of the draug."

I looked around. Jewels was chewing her lip as she thought about it. Sam had sort of a that-might-be-a-good-idea look on his face. I turned back to Cristof, "Well, why don't we go see Lilah. We can ask her about it and find out the progress on the Directors Meeting."

~

We were ushered into Lilah's office without delay. She was on a tell with another Director, but she soon finished and came around her desk. "Oh, Joshua, it's so good to see you." She hugged him and kissed his cheek, and I felt a pang of jealousy. I tried to swallow the emotion, but I saw the look on Jewels's face.

"Quit eavesdropping," I hissed at her. She just rolled her eyes and shook her head.

"Lilah," Cristof said. "Betty, Jewels, and Sam have filled me in on their activity since arriving. But, how have you been holding up?"

"It's getting bad, Joshua," Lilah said returning to her seat. We sat with her around her desk. "Money's tight and my workers are suffering. I'm trying to help as much as I can, but there's nothing I can do with the fishing drying up."

"Well, now, I do have a couple of ideas for you," Cristof said. "First, I will contact my bank. I believe we can offer you a short-term loan at reasonable rates. I know you will do everything in your power to pay off the loan. Second, I wanted to ask whether you had considered raising bluefin in tanks, rather than just trying to catch wild fish."

Lilah looked puzzled. "I'm not sure I'm following..."

"You see, I have this idea that you could create—well, sort of like holding pens, in the water, and put the bluefin you are catching into the pens and let them breed naturally and then just sort of scoop them out as needed."

"I don't..." Lilah began, then stopped. "I...it might work. We could...I need to talk to some people about this. It's...it doesn't seem natural, but maybe it could work. Sort of like farming the fish."

"Exactly!" Cristof beamed. "I'm sure it will take some work and a lot of trial and error to get things going, but the loan from me will help cover the costs and, if you are successful, you will have no problems with the loan or the future of your fishing operation."

"Mary!" Lilah called out, not bothering to use her tell. Mrs. Kyle poked her head inside the door. "Get Morgan's team together and have them here in my office in half an hour. No excuses. Tell them to bring everything they've got on bluefin so far."

"Yes, ma'am." Mrs. Kyle hurried back to her desk.

"Thank you so much, Joshua. What else can I do for you?"

"Ah, I believe Mr. Sterling has some questions for you."

"Yes." I cleared my throat. "We understand the importance of the Directors Meeting, but we think Sam and Jewels and I should investigate the draug more closely. Specifically, we want to find the tech controlling the draug, 'cause that should finally lead us to whoever is behind these events. We thought you could help us figure out a way to track the tech."

During my brief oration, Lilah's elation from Cristof's idea had fallen from her face, and she now looked worried. She gazed over our heads, deep in thought, and we didn't want to break the silence. Finally she looked at me with haunted eyes. "Betty... can I see what happened?"

I started getting nervous. "What, exactly, do you mean?"

She hesitated. "I need to find out exactly what was going on when you met the draug. I've only heard your story and I think I need to experience the real thing. So...I wanted to see your memories?" She made it a plaintive query.

Jewels looked alarmed. "You can't ask him to do that! You can't go that deep."

"I know, Jewels, but...I need to know exactly what was happening. It might provide clues to figure out how to track down the trollman behind this."

"I've heard 'think' and 'might,' but you don't know, and it's too much to ask Betty to do that."

"I'll decide if it's too much, Jewels." I looked over at Cristof, but he just sat silently, one eyebrow raised as if he thought the whole thing slightly academic. I looked back at Lilah, who had a pleading look on her face. I had never had a telepath go into my memories before and it scared me. Because it was Lilah, it also excited me, and that scared me even more.

Jewels yelled at me, "Betty! She's a troll! How can you even think that?"

I got really irritated. "You're eavesdropping again, Jewels, and that is far worse than anything I've been thinking."

Cristof finally interrupted by clearing his throat. "Yes, well, I think the two of you," he looked at Lilah and me, "need some privacy. Jewels, let's go outside and keep Sam company." He rose and headed for the door, looking pointedly at Jewels.

Jewels glowered at me. "I can't believe you're even considering it, Betty. And with a cat." She sneered the last word directly at Lilah, and I saw the hurt in Lilah's eyes as I bit off a retort in kind. With one last glare, Jewels spun on her heel and marched past Cristof. He smiled apologetically at both of us and closed the door as he stepped out.

I turned back to Lilah. "I've never done this before. Uh...how does it work?"

She tried to smile, but the worry on her face chased it away. "Just relax. Close your eyes and let your mind wander back to when you first encountered the draug. I'll have to touch you in order to join your thoughts."

I nodded, leaned back in my chair and closed my eyes. I heard Lilah come around her desk and pull up a chair opposite me. She sat so our knees were just touching and took both my hands with hers. I settled down and tried to focus on the events from a few days ago. I felt pressure building in my head, like a headache was beginning to form right behind my eyes, and I squinted against the pain. It suddenly disappeared.

"You're fighting me, Betty. Just relax, and let my thoughts join yours."

I took a deep breath and tried to relax my whole body. I focused on my memories again and felt the pressure building. This time, instead of trying to push back, I tried to open my head to the pressure. Suddenly it released and I felt Lilah's presence in my mind; at the same time, I felt nauseated.

It was not so much a sense of Lilah there with me, but it was as if I was Lilah and Lilah was me...yeah, I can't explain it very well. I was two people, and it was worse than being seasick. The events from Bluth streamed through my mind and I could see the shambling corpses, and hear the crack of Sam's staff, and smell the burning char. Then it was over. Lilah's presence was gone, and I leaned over the arm of my chair and threw up.

I sat there, bent over, gasping for air and trying not to retch again. Lilah finally managed a weak, "Thank you, Betty," and I sat up enough to see her. She had leaned back in her chair and covered her face with her hands and was pressing hard on her forehead as though trying to shove herself back into her own mind. "Oh," she muttered. "That gives me the most awful headache."

She finally sat forward, reached out and grasped my shoulders. "We'll talk later. I've got to get myself together before my fish experts come in. I'll come see you at the inn. You had better go rest."

I nodded weakly, pushed myself upright and headed toward the door. As I was leaving, I turned to Mrs. Kyle and told her, "You might want to get a janitor in there. Soon." She looked at me quizzically and then hurried into the office. I shuffled my way down the hall, feeling a little like a draug myself.

NINE

The argument between Jewels and me started almost as soon as I woke up. Cristof and Jewels had gotten me to the inn and into bed, but any time they tried to ask questions, I just shook my head and concentrated on keeping my body up and my food down. I slept for a couple of hours and woke feeling, not refreshed, but at least not as sick. Jewels had drawn the task of watching over me. I soon discovered that was a mistake.

She started in as soon as she was sure I wasn't still suffering. "I can't believe you let her do that, Betty. Joining like that should only be between two telepaths who can both control it. You're lucky she didn't kill you."

"She wouldn't kill me," I retorted. "She likes me." Jewels snorted. "She likes *all* of us. She doesn't want to hurt us or want us to get hurt, and she wants to help us. She *has* helped us. A lot. And anyway, if two telepaths could do it, why didn't you offer to take my place?"

"I wouldn't let her into my mind!"

"Wow, big surprise. I wonder how she managed to figure that out."

"Just because you're in love with her doesn't mean I have to like her."

"I'm not in love with her. Yes, I like her, but it's not love."

"Go ahead and keep telling yourself that, but don't try to put it over on me. I know what I see. I know what I've heard when you're thinking out loud."

"And that's another thing. I know you have to focus to hear people, so why do you keep eavesdropping on me? It's bad enough knowing strangers can be out there picking my brain, knowing one of my friends is doing it kinda chafes me."

"I like to keep tabs on you to make sure you're not going to do something stupid," Jewels retorted.

"Oh, so you think I'm likely to do something stupid? Thanks for the vote of confidence."

"Actually, I'm starting to think this whole thing is stupid. What are we doing here, Betty? Chasing after fish-snatchers? That's no kind of job. Let these people deal with their own problems. They probably just over-fished anyway."

"'Fish-snatchers?' We've gone way beyond worrying about fish. What about those walking corpses?"

"Yeah, what about them? They scare me, OK? I don't want to have anything more to do with them, or the stinking fish, or your precious Miss Cat!"

"Stop calling her that!"

"What do you want me to call her? A troll?! How's that. How about I call her a troll, 'cause she is. She's a dirty troll and you can't trust her..."

"How about you call her a person," I hissed,

"because she is. She's just as much a person as me or you or Sam."

"Trolls aren't people, Betty. They look like animals and most of 'em act like animals..."

"Lilah doesn't," I cut in. "She looks almost the same as a human and she certainly doesn't act like an animal."

"So? Just because she cleaned herself up doesn't mean she isn't still a troll. You're letting yourself get drawn to her and you're forgetting what she is."

"Why do you care what I feel about her? What difference does it make to you?"

"I don't want to see you get mixed up with a cat. Like I said, I listen in so you don't do something stupid."

"So you don't like her, you don't like the way I feel about her, you think I'm being stupid, and you don't like the mission. So why are you still here? Why don't you go home?"

"Well then," Jewels answered, "when we get to Braysport, I'll take the Tube home. You obviously don't need me anymore."

"What I don't need is your nasty attitude about Lilah and about her problems. I need your help, but I need you to want to help."

"Well, if that's what you want...don't hold your breath." Jewels stalked from the room.

Way to go, Betty, I thought. I need Jewels's technical ability, but I'm chasing her off...why? Just because she doesn't approve of Lilah? Why should her approval matter to me?

Because, she's my friend, I answered myself. And

she's my partner on this mission. I need her support to finish what we started here. And that's more important than whatever I'm feeling for Lilah.

Is she right? OK, I am attracted to Lilah, but it's not love. I'm old enough to know what love feels like and this isn't it. I think. Ugh. I need Jewels, but I also need... WE...also need Lilah's help. Somehow I've got to patch this up enough to get them working together. I can worry about whether they actually like each other later. Or maybe never. Once this mission is over, it probably becomes a moot point anyway. It's not like Lilah's going to leave her Hold and move to Fisk, and I'm not moving down here to the middle of nowhere.

No, when this is over, it's over. I'm a hired enforcer, Lilah's a business director, and Jewels is my friend and a part of my team. It's not like I don't have enough to deal with right now. I sighed again. Time to go see Jewels and cool her down. I rose and found I was still a little unsteady on my feet. I stood still a moment taking deep, slow breaths, and while I was standing there was a knock at the door.

"Yes?" I called.

"It's Lilah."

I got myself to the door under my own power and opened it. I admit I was using the door to hold myself up.

She smiled at me. "How are you doing?"

"I'm still a little woozy, but I'll get over it."

"I'm so sorry." She reached out a hand to touch my cheek, but quickly pulled it back. "Are you ready to talk about it?"

"Yeah, but we need to track down the others." I

started to go through the door, but she put a hand to my chest.

"I'll go find them. You stay here and I'll bring them to you."

I smiled as thanks and went and found a chair and slumped into it. I wondered if Jewels would even bother answering the door, especially to Lilah. It wasn't long before Lilah returned, with Cristof and Sam in tow. Straggling in behind Cristof, almost as if being pulled, came Jewels.

I stood up and looked at Jewels. She was still angry. I knew it was probably going to cost me, but I squatted down and put myself at her level. Her eyes softened a little.

"Jewels. I'm sorry. I need your help...I need your help now and I'll need it again in the future. Whatever my personal feelings about anything else, it's more important that I have your support. You're the best tech I know," her face brightened a little, "and I can't do this job without you. I would have failed at a lot of jobs over the years without your help. Will you stay and help now?"

Jewels craned her neck around and looked at Cristof and he nodded encouragingly at her. She turned back to me. "OK, Betty. I'll stay and help." She paused and then took a deep breath. "And I'll try not to listen anymore." It wasn't exactly an apology, but I'd take it. For now.

Cristof beamed and rubbed his hands together. "Excellent! Now, let's get down to business. Jewels, could you ward us, please?" Jewels nodded and concentrated for a moment. I couldn't sense any change, but after a moment she said, "Done."

Lilah took over. "First, thank you Betty for allowing me to see what happened in Bluth. After thinking over the experience, I don't think we're dealing with draug." She paused as we all murmured in surprise. "For one thing, none of the...whatever they are... showed any decay. A trollman can raise the dead, but can't stop them from decomposing. Unless all those people had been killed in the last few days, some of them should have started to rot." I retched a little thinking of that and clamped down. That was not a feeling I needed right now.

Lilah continued. "For another thing there has to be more than one trollman. No one person could control that many things. But they were definitely under control. They were acting with intelligence. If I can get next to an animated one without its controller being aware of me, I might be able to trace him down before he can sever the connection."

"You'd be wide open to counterattack if you tried that." Surprisingly, it was Jewels who objected. "You wouldn't be of any help if you had your mind destroyed."

"If I were fast enough, he wouldn't have time to react."

"Can you be that fast? I couldn't."

"Well, is there some way you could back me up? Maybe if you shielded me while..."

Jewels shook her head. "Nope. If I were shielding you, you wouldn't be able to read your own trace."

Lilah and Jewels both lapsed into silence. I had no idea what they were talking about, so I kept quiet. It was Sam who finally broke in. "Excuse me, but can you confirm the trollman who is controlling these—what shall we call them?"

"Let's just use 'draug' for now. Maybe that's not what they are, but it's the only word we've got."

"Very good, Betty. The trollman controlling the draug sees through their eyes and hears through their ears?"

Lilah nodded. "Yes. As I understand it, he can see and hear through the draug."

"And you need to approach a draug without being detected and then you have a brief moment when you can trace the controller's thought. But, if you do not act swiftly enough, the controller could close the connection or even use it to attack you telepathically."

Jewels cut in, "Exactly. She'd be wide open while trying to trace down the controller."

"Well then," said Sam, "what we need to do is create a distraction that disorients the controller. That would allow us to get close to the draug and trace the controller before he is aware of what is happening."

"How do we do that?" I asked.

"Give me some time to work on a solution."

"There's something else we need to settle, then." Jewels put in. "I should do the tracking."

"Why you?" I asked.

"Because I'm the tech on this team and she's the client. I can do the job and she needs to go to her Directors Meeting."

"You're all going." Lilah said. "We need your report of what happened in Bluth."

"You've seen it yourself now. You can provide the

report. Betty, Sam, and I should head straight to Bluth and figure this thing out."

"Actually, Jewels, going to the Directors Meeting would be a good thing." Sam put out a hand as she started to object. "I have an idea of how to create a distraction, but I need to work on it, and, if I recall correctly, Ms. Burkah, one of the directors is an elf who runs a technology company?"

"Yes," Lilah said. "Prizm runs an elven enclave that makes mostly telepathic equipment."

"We will need to see her. Unless either you or Jewels can meld spells?" Both ladies shook their heads.

"Good!" I had almost forgotten Cristof was in the room with us. "It's settled. You will all travel to the Directors Meeting tomorrow and I will return to Fisk. It seems you're heading in the right direction, so I'll let you get on with your work."

Lilah went over and hugged him. "Thank you so much for your help, Joshua. I'll keep you posted on the progress we're making on those fish farms."

I stepped over and shook Cristof's hand. "Thanks. I know we're not, strictly speaking, chasing fish thieves anymore, but..."

"Oh, no," Cristof interrupted, "what you're doing now is more important, and may lead to solving everyone's problems before you're finished." He squatted down and put out a hand to Jewels. She approached slowly and took it. "And you'll think more on what we talked about, yes?"

Jewels just nodded, a little sullenly, I thought.

"Great! I'm already packed and I'll have my driver take me now. Good luck to all of you, and if you need any more help, just send me a message." Cristof smiled at all of us and took his leave. I turned to look at Jewels.

"What did you and Cristof talk about?"

"None of your business, Betty."

TEN

The following morning, after a brief discussion, we decided to all travel to Braysport on *Sea Lily*. A tell with Captain Spanner revealed the ship had been running low on supplies and it was too much of a burden on Darfa to restock there. Braysport would have docks big enough for an ogre-sized ship and plenty of stores Spanner could buy for the extended stay this had turned into. The journey would take slightly longer than by floater, but still less than a day.

I didn't eat much for breakfast.

Braysport had been one of our stops on the trip to Darfa, but I hadn't paid it much attention then. The trip back didn't make me nearly as sick as previous trips on *Sea Lily*, and I even ate a decent lunch. As we were disembarking at Braysport, I commented that I seemed to be getting my "sea legs."

Lilah pulled me aside and whispered in my ear, "Don't get too cocky. I've been suppressing your nausea the whole trip." She smiled, patted my cheek, and headed down the passerelle to the pier. Great. I'm surrounded by women who can read my mind and even manipulate me without my noticing. Maybe I need to start wearing my gold-weaved hood all the time.

As a trade center, most of the public buildings in Braysport were built to ogre specifications. The host of the meeting, Dylan Murphrie, had sent a couple of over-sized floaters to pick us up from the docks. As we headed toward our transport, I noted the lack of fishing vessels in port. Everything seemed to either be a cargo ship or personal boat like *Sea Lily*.

"Dylan's a trader," Lilah explained. "Cargo is unloaded here for shipment overland, or loaded from overland transports onto ships for destinations around the world. He's strictly a facilitator. He doesn't produce anything himself. Most of our fish go through here." She paused. "When we were catching fish," and she lapsed into a brooding silence.

I put an arm on her shoulders, "We'll figure out what's going on and we'll stop it. You'll be back in business in no time." She smiled up at me and nestled into me, turning my friendly arm into a full hug. I felt warmth in the pit of my stomach and, getting suddenly nervous, stepped away and tried to cover up the moment.

"What's the program now that we're here?" I tried to sound gruff and business-like.

Lilah raised her eyebrows at me when I suddenly stepped away, but she smiled as though she knew something I didn't. "Nothing tonight. The meeting officially starts tomorrow, so we're free to check into our rooms and get something to eat."

"I would like to meet with Prizm tonight, if possible," Sam said. "I am anxious to know if my idea is feasible."

"Let's go, then," Lilah said. "I'll contact Prizm and see if she'll have dinner with us."

~

Prizm was an elf of average height, which meant she was a couple of spans taller than Jewels, and her hair and eyes were a lighter shade of lavender. She had three other elves with her, a woman and two men, introduced as Sapphire, Facet, and Ruby. Elvish naming convention always leaves me slightly amused. So does their riot of clashing hair and eye colors, like the lavender, orange, green, and yellow I found myself staring at now.

Surprisingly, Jewels looked askance at the group of her own people sitting across from her and didn't seem intent on ingratiating herself with them. I leaned down and whispered, "What's wrong?"

"Mechanics," she whispered back, somehow putting a world of sarcasm into that one word. "They're nothing but hacks melding spells into metal instead of using real tech."

Oh great, I thought, we found another one of Jewels's prejudices. "Well, keep your feelings to yourself. Sam seems to need their help, so be nice even if it kills you."

She looked up at me and gave me a totally fake, wide-eyed grin. "Like this?" I just grunted at her.

The formality of introductions aside and dinner ordered, Sam launched into his idea. "What I am looking for is a device that can cast a combination of spells, but only after a delay of several breaths."

The elves seemed taken aback at the notion. "You mean," said Prizm, "you want to meld more than one spell into a disc, then, when you focus on it, only have the spells activate AFTER you focus on it, rather than at the same time as you focus on it?"

"Exactly! Can it be done?"

The green-haired male elf rather arbitrarily named Ruby rubbed his jaw. "The first thing we'd have to do is figure out how to combine spells. Have we ever made anything that had two spells melded together?"

The others shook their heads, but then Facet, a girl with lemon-yellow hair and eyes piped up, "Would having two separate devices work?"

Sam considered a moment, "I cannot see why not. The idea is to have two—or possibly more—spells go off together. They would not have to be in the same actual disc, but they would need to be together."

Prizm jumped back in, "Let's get back to the delayed activation. Spells normally activate when you focus on them. Sapphire, you're the expert on activation, can it be done?"

Sapphire's orange eyes looked worried. "I can't even begin to figure out how. Spells are a matter of thought and how do you delay thought?"

"That's it!" Facet clapped her hands together. "You need another spell—a 'thought' spell."

"You may be right," Sapphire said. "You could have one spell activate another." He fished a piece of paper and a pencil from his pocket. "You would need two discs for each spell. Say you wanted to cast an ice spell and a fire spell at the same time—though I don't know why, as they would just cancel each other out—but, say you did. You have one disc with a fire spell and one disc with an ice spell. Then you need one disc that

activates the fire disc and one disc that activates the
ice disc." He was drawing little discs stacked on top of
one another and marking each one as he spoke. "The
activation discs would need to simulate thought that
counts down, say from five to one and then activates
the spell on its related disc."

"Hold on a minute," Prizm interjected. "We've
never tried having one melded object activate another
melded object. Normally the owner has to be in contact
with the device in order to force it to activate. Plus
we've never tried putting thought on a disc."

"Telepaths imprint discs all the time. Why couldn't
a telepath imprint an activation on a disc?" queried
Lilah while poring over the drawings with the elves.

"Yeah, but how is the thought disc going to own
the spell disc?" Prizm obviously relished her place as
raiser of objections.

"You bond the spell disc to the thought disc and
then bond the thought discs to the owner, so the
owner could activate the thought discs, then after the
countdown, the main spells would go off."

"Guys," Jewels interjected, "you're making this too
complicated. Put the activation spell on a wand, then
you can fire it from a distance."

"Yeah, but then what about the delay?"

"Do you need a delay if you can choose when to set
it off?"

"That could possibly work," Sam admitted. "The
idea behind the delay was to allow you to activate the
spells and then throw them at your target. If you used
a wand to set off the spells, you could just use a wand
to cast the spells, and I wanted a solution that avoided

line-of-sight."

"Why do you need to avoid line-of-sight? Don't you need to see the target to throw something at it?"

"Well, I wanted spells that would momentarily blind and deafen the target without blinding and deafening me."

"So you throw the spell package, then duck out of sight to shield yourself from the effect? Yeah, let's go back to the original idea. Activation spell melded to one disc sets off the spell on the other disc. Can we try that?" Prizm looked around at her team. They all nodded. "OK, we'll get to work on it after we get home." She looked at Sam, "This won't be cheap, customized gear like this. Now, what spells did you want in the package?"

"The spells need to disorient and confuse while also momentarily blinding and deafening the target. I was thinking of some kind of very bright light and very high-pitched sound."

Ruby shrugged his shoulders, "Banshee wail and a standard light spell cranked up. But you'll need to wear ear plugs and some type of eye shield or you'll also be affected."

"We'll worry about that," I said, "you just worry about making that package." I could see where Sam was going and thought it was a good idea. If we threw this package among a group of draug, the feedback to the trollman would hurt and give Jewels time to trace back the connection. "And don't worry about the expense. We can cover it."

I sighed. Those two thousand marks sure were disappearing fast.

ELEVEN

The Directors Meeting started and ended the next day. In fact, the whole thing from our end was a disaster. Jewels, Sam, and I never testified. We knew something was wrong when we walked into the meeting room and saw Taylor Harris chatting with a couple of the other directors. He looked a lot livelier than the last time I saw him burning and falling into a hole I had made.

Lilah covered pretty well, but it was clear she was embarrassed. She had called everyone together because of a terrible situation in Bluth and here was Director Harris telling everyone everything was fine and he had no idea what terrible thing might have caused Director Burkah to call a meeting. Lilah shooed us out and went back in to take her medicine and sit through whatever else the directors wanted to talk about while they were all together.

The mood was gloomy that evening. We sat in the room assigned to Sam and me and kind of just stared at each other.

"So," I finally broke the silence. "What do we do now? We all know what we saw, but Harris isn't as dead as we thought and no one is going to believe anything different. To be honest, I'm starting to doubt myself. I think we're being duped."

"No." Lilah was emphatic. "We're going ahead as planned. I'll take the Tube tomorrow to Prizm's enclave and work out your spell package, Sam. You three will go back to Darfa and sit tight. Once we have that package, we'll all head for Bluth and find out what's going on. Taylor is obviously involved. That makes me very mad, and I'm going to do something about it."

"You're supposed to stay out of this," Jewels objected. "I thought we agreed I was going to trace the tech."

"*I* don't remember agreeing to that." Lilah stressed the '*I*.' "This is my business and my fight and, frankly, Jewels, I'm a better telepath than you, so I can do the job quicker."

Jewels stared at Lilah for a moment then looked away. "Yeah, you got me there. But you two did *not* hear me just admit that." And she glared at Sam and me.

The trip back to Darfa wasn't nearly as pleasant as the trip to Braysport. Without Lilah there to damp the nausea, I spent the whole trip in my bunk with occasional trips to the head to heave up what little I had left in my stomach. When we finally reached Darfa, Captain Spanner himself took us in to shore; he wanted to speak to some of the local fishermen.

"I was going to talk to the director," he explained, "but she didn't come back with us. So I thought I'd ask some of the locals about the huge seaport that's been built on one of the islands out in the middle of the

Arran Sea."

"There's a seaport out there?"

"Aye, Mr. Sterling. My crew and I saw it while we were exploring during your trip into the mountains. There's a string of islands running from the southern end of the Arran into the middle of the Sea. Most are tiny things and my maps indicate no habitations on any of them. But while we were cruising past the end-most isles, we spied quite a busy seaport on one of them. We could only see it well with our glass and we couldn't tell what they were doing, just that there was a lot of activity."

"Why would someone build a seaport in the middle of the sea, where there are no roads or a Tube station?" Sam wondered.

"That was my question, as well," answered Spanner. "One I was hopin' would be answered by the director or one of her captains." He doffed his cap at us and headed off toward a group of fishermen working on their boat. Sam and I stared at each other.

"The missing bluefin?" Sam finally asked.

"Maybe," I answered, "but we've got a bigger problem with this Bluth mess. Let's deal with that, and then I think we all go take a closer look at that seaport. But...why would anyone build a seaport in the middle of the ocean?"

~

I won't bore you with the details of what Sam, Jewels, and I did over the next four days until Lilah returned. Suffice it to say the only thing I accomplished was losing a few marks to the other two in friendly card games. After two days of sitting on my duff, I was about ready to jump on *Sea Lily* and go take a look at that mysterious seaport; only the thought of more days of seasickness kept me from following through.

Finally, Lilah returned and came to our inn. "Here it is," she said, holding out a small clinking bag once Jewels had warded the room. "A package of spell discs just like you asked for, Sam. They bonded the activation discs to me. All I have to do it focus on it, then you throw it and they go off. You've got about ten breaths to get rid of it once I activate it."

"Shouldn't it be inside a protective sheath?" I asked.

"I can control my focus a lot better than you, Betty. It's not going off until I'm ready for it to go off."

"How much did it cost?"

"They wanted two hundred, but I talked them down to half that. I said they could use the process to make more spell packs and market them and the profits would cover their costs. They bought it, and we bought this." She tucked the bag through her belt.

"Great," I said, "I just started an arms race. You realize they'll put more destructive spells on the ones they sell, right?"

"Yeah, well, people go around killing people anyway," Jewels said. "Does it really matter how they do it?"

Lilah interrupted our philosophical debate before we could get rolling. "We'll be ready first thing in the morning. We're not going to sneak in this time. I've lined up a group of police and we're going to take floaters in over the main road. We'll reach Bluth in a few hours. If all goes well, we can be in and out and back in Darfa by dinner time."

I looked up at the sun. Another half-day of waiting.

~

The convoy of floaters pulled up just around a bend in the road, out of sight of the town of Bluth. Lilah had filled us in on the plan during the trip. We planned to march into town in full view of whomever or whatever was there. If everything really was all right, as Harris had said at the Directors Meeting, then we would turn around and go home. If we found the draug there, the advance of an armed force would cause the trollmen to confront us. We would deploy our spell package, Lilah would trace one of the trollmen, and we would hunt him down to get answers.

To a point, the plan worked beautifully. The four of us, backed up by a score of Darfa police, marched down the road and into Bluth. The draug were there, shuffling back and forth to the mine, just as we had seen on our previous visit. It took them a moment to react to our presence and they began clumping up and heading our way. Captain Graisson steadied his force and Lilah, Sam, Jewels, and I ran off to the side, getting behind some buildings and looking for a still-isolated group of draug.

From the direction of the road we could hear the police yelling and wands exploding. We crept through an alley and spied a small group of four draug shuffling toward the fray. Lilah looked around and mouthed, "Now." We all stuck plugs of fabric in our ears as she pulled out the spell bag and focused on it, then gave it to Sam, who chucked it out in front of the draug. We all turned away and closed our eyes.

The elves had outdone themselves. Even with the ear plugs, the wail that screamed its way into the sky made my head hurt and left me briefly disoriented. We could also see the bright flash of light even with our backs turned, our eyes closed and partially shielded by the building we were hiding behind. As soon as the wailing stopped, we all turned and sped around the corner. Sam, Jewels, and I were to keep any approaching draug off Lilah while she worked on one of the draug close to the blast.

We weren't needed. Sam's spell bag had done the trick. The draug everywhere had simply collapsed as whoever was controlling them had been put out of action by the blast. Lilah sped ahead, hissing, and leaped at the nearest draug, grabbing its head and focusing her mind on whatever trace of a mental link still existed between it and its controller. The tableau seemed frozen in my mind and stretched on for an eternity—or about fifteen breaths—and then Lilah was walking back toward us with a strange look on her face.

"Let's go," she said and started walking back toward her police force.

"What is it?" I asked.

"Not now," she replied tersely. "We'll go over everything once we get back to Darfa, but as I thought, these are not draug. They're constructs. Wooden statues brought to life by some very powerful tech. Captain!" She called out brusquely as we approached the police. "These things are made out of wood. Set fire to this place. There is no one living here and I want to send a message to Mr. Harris." She managed to twist the name into a word of spite.

Graisson saluted and set about sending those of his force with fire wands around to set fire to everything. I pulled out my own fire wand and was going to join them, when Lilah put her hand on my arm. "Wait, Betty. Let's move over here and talk for a moment."

The four of us stepped away into a small huddle. "I don't understand how it's being done, but the trollmen who are controlling these constructs are not here. They're far away. I couldn't get a good fix before they started pushing back, but...I know this sounds crazy, but I got the impression they were in the middle of the Arran Sea."

Sam and I looked at each other. I turned back to Lilah, "I know just where to go. Or, I should say, Captain Spanner knows where to go. He discovered...what was *that*?" The noise sounded like a rockfall, the sound of rock striking rock and grinding against each other. A couple of the police came running from between the burning buildings.

"Monster!" was all they yelled and kept going. Graisson yelled at them, and then started yelling at all of his force to form up. The four of us hurried back over to join them and watched as something came from the direction of the mine.

It was huge, easily three times the size of Sam, and it was made entirely of rock. It was bearing down on us with surprising speed, covering huge chunks of ground with each step. While vaguely human-shaped, it had no face or even what could be called a head. It was just four limbs attached to a massive rock torso and it made no sound other than the sound of its component rocks rubbing each other.

I whipped out my nature wand and aimed a stone-dissolving blast at the thing's left leg. The spell fizzled out a few spans away from the body. It was shielded. "Scatter!" I yelled, and grabbed Lilah's arm and dragged her with me.

"Let go! What are you doing? I don't need you to protect me!"

"I'm not protecting you," I hissed through clenched teeth. "We can't fight this thing if all our tech won't work. I'm going to get you inside the shield and you're going to attack whoever is controlling it. It's the only chance we've got."

"I'm going in, too." That's when I noticed Jewels was levitating right behind us. I didn't have time to argue, but just grunted and continued running behind the thing, assuming it had a backside at all.

I could hear explosions from the other side of the monster, proof that Captain Graisson had enough of a head on his shoulders to order his troops to fire outside the shield. I doubted any conventional spells were going to do much against a massive, moving wall of rock. You might as well try to fight an avalanche.

I ripped my hood off my head and dropped it, hoping I would be able to find it again, then I cast a thought out, "Are you both listening?" In my head I 'heard' both Lilah and Jewels answer. "Then follow what I'm thinking." I stuck my fire wand in my belt, raised the nature wand and drew a gully in front of the monster. It tripped and stumbled, briefly dropping to one 'knee' and its 'hands' hit the ground.

I grabbed Lilah around the waist, picked her up and ran full tilt toward the back of the monster. I leaped on the bent leg and began clambering up the rocks. "Let me go, I can climb," echoed in my head, so I released Lilah. "We've got to find its head, whatever that might be," I thought aloud. Jewels was levitating past us now, trying to find the control point for the monster.

The creature was pushing itself erect. The movement caused me to lose my grip and I briefly hung by a few fingers and toes. Grunting with the effort, I swung my body around, crashing into the creature and scrabbling for another handhold. My free hand found a small outcropping and grabbed on while I jammed my foot deeper into a crevice between two rocks. Then the monster shifted and the rocks crushed my foot.

I screamed in pain, let go with my wand hand and aimed a blast with the nature wand downward, in the general direction of my leg. It was an instinctive reaction; I hadn't even considered I was inside the shield. The nature wand dissolved a hole right through the thing's leg. The monster stumbled forward and fell. I lost my grip completely and fell among the crashing rocks. I was several lengths above the ground and falling flat. I tried to twist around so I wouldn't pancake the ground when something hit me, hard, and knocked me away from the crashing debris of the monster.

I suddenly found myself hanging in the air, wrapped up by someone, then the two of us began floating toward the ground. I put my hands and knees down as I came near the ground and knelt there, panting. Lilah was still on my back, her arms wrapped around my belly, and she didn't seem ready to let go. "Get off!" I wheezed. "My foot!"

She abruptly rolled off and I collapsed with a groan, rolling over onto my back. Above me I could see Jewels floating down. She had her hands wrapped around a metal sphere. I struggled into a sitting position and looked down at my right boot. I couldn't see any blood, but I began struggling with the straps, trying to get it off.

Lilah moved over and helped me, but as soon as she began tugging at the boot, I screamed. "No! That hurts too much. Leave it!"

"What happened?" Jewels asked.

"My foot got caught in between two rocks. Can you scry it?"

"I don't do that kind of scrying, Betty. We'll have to get you to a doctor."

I looked at Lilah, but she mutely shook her head and looked at my foot. I closed my eyes and tried to block out the throbbing pain shooting in waves up my leg. I became aware of other noises—the sounds of Lilah's police force calling to each other, rocks still rolling here and there, and the crackle of flames from the burning buildings of Bluth.

"I need to go check on my people," Lilah said. I opened my eyes as she stood and tried to smile at her, but it probably looked more like a grimace.

I looked over at Jewels, "Where's Sam?"

Jewels's eyes went unfocused and then she pointed into Bluth, which was still burning. "He's in there. He's torching buildings."

"We'll let him do that, then. What's that?" I pointed at the metal sphere Jewels was cradling.

"It's the control mechanism for the construct," she answered. "We found it embedded in the top of that thing. It's how they were animating it and able to see and hear everything. Miss Cat—Lilah—put a 'pathic shield around it and cut 'em off. That was about the same time you blew a hole in its leg, so it just collapsed."

"Will there be more of them?"

"I don't know, but I think if they had more they would have already attacked."

I stared out at the burning town. Nothing was moving. "They still have to have the wooden people-looking things in there. If they haven't brought those running, it means they've probably given Bluth up as a lost cause...unnh," I grunted as a fresh wave of pain from my foot ran through my body.

"I'm sorry, Betty. I wish I could do something for you...hey! There's Sam."

Sam was trudging out of the town. He stopped some distance from us, stooped, and picked up something from the ground. Approaching, he wordlessly held out my hood and sat down beside us.

"I knew I would be no help batting at that thing with my staff, so I decided to run into town. I lit my staff on one of the already-burning buildings and then used it to set everything else I could find on fire. When we get home, Betty, you owe me a new staff."

"The nicest one I can find, Sam."

We sat there in silence, listening to the crackle of flames from Bluth, until Lilah returned. "We lost four policemen, including David Graisson," she said in a tight, controlled voice. "Let's get back to Darfa."

"What about the bodies of the police?"

Lilah turned and looked at what remained of the construct. "They're already buried. Under that." She was grinding her teeth as she spoke. "When I catch up with Harris, he's going to wish he'd been buried with them."

TWELVE

The trip back to Darfa was slow and solemn. Lilah sat beside me, resting her hand on my forehead, helping to block the pain. From the grimacing on her face, it seemed part of what I was feeling was leaking through to her. I tried to smile up at her. "I never properly thanked you for helping with my seasickness."

She looked down at me. "That was nothing. You're really not all that sick, it's just...once something like that starts, it becomes an automatic reaction. This pain, though...close your eyes and rest. It will make it easier for me."

I did as I was told, and when we reached Darfa, I was sent straight to a doctor. The prognosis was multiple broken bones in my foot. The doctor recommended a soft wrap and several weeks of bed rest, but that wasn't going to work. After arguing with Lilah for a while, the doctor grudgingly agreed to use a stasis boot. I'd be able to walk. Sort of.

The next day we had a conference at the inn. Captain Spanner was there. We also included Lieutenant Fitzgerald, interim commanding officer of Lilah's police force, and Captain Brevery, one of the senior captains in the fishing fleet. Captain Spanner kicked things off with a description of the seaport he had seen while cruising.

Pointing to a map of the area, Spanner began, "As you know, the Sea of Arran isn't a proper ocean, more like a large bay or gulf. It separates the continents of Ilanerra and Gorsj. To the south is a narrow land connection between the two continents and from that area, a string of small islands extends north into the Arran Sea. Most of these islands are little more than rocks rising out of the sea, smaller than your average farm, though some are a few furlongs on each side.

"Some days ago, my men and I spied something on the northernmost islands in the chain. Using a glass, we saw a seaport with ships moving in and out. We stayed out away from the port, as our charts showed nothing should be in that area, and we were concerned about pirates. I reported what we found to Cap'n Brevery and I'll turn it over to him to continue."

"Thank ye, Cap'n Spanner. The main shipping lanes are to the north of here and there isn't much sea traffic along our coast and south except for the fishing boats and the occasional charter such as Cap'n Spanner runs. So I was mighty interested in what might be happenin' out in the middle of the Sea. I found some lads as had been in-and-out of those islands in their youth and sent 'em out to survey the area."

He tipped his head toward Lilah. "Beggin' yer pardon, ma'am, we sent 'em out at night so as not to be seen." Lilah gave him a tight smile and nodded at him to continue. "The ships I sent out returned just yesterday. They sailed in some ways south of the port

Cap'n Spanner reported and made their way north with masts unstepped and moving by oar around the islands. They found the port right enough and spied on 'em for better than a day a'fore creeping south and sailin' for home."

Brevery took a deep breath before continuing, "If I didn't trust these men with my own life, I'd not believe what they told me. Several of the northern isles have been joined by breakwaters to form a harbor and transport ships are coming in and goin' out like clockwork. But they also seen a ship—maybe more than one—come up OUT of the water and cruise into the harbor, be unloaded, and then cruise out again and disappear UNDER the water. Somethin' greatly unnatural is goin' on out there, ma'am."

Lilah's natural frown had deepened during Brevery's oration and the room sat in silence for several moments after he finished. Finally she looked at Brevery, "Recommendations, Captain?"

"Beggin' yer pardon again, ma'am, we're just fishermen. We've got no ships to be fightin' other ships with. And we don't really know what they're doing or who they are."

"I know who they are, Captain. They're the people who attacked us in Bluth. This is where the telepathic signal was coming from, though I have no clue how they were reaching that far. But you are right about the fact we have no ships to fight with. That's why you and I are going to Gorsj. We're going to hire ourselves a navy." She turned to her new police commander. "Lieutenant, you must get every able-bodied person in this Hold ready for a fight. I'm issuing a militia order today and you've got only a few days to ready our people. We don't know what we'll be facing, but the incident in Bluth gives us a good idea of what they can do."

Fitzgerald swallowed nervously and said, "Yes, ma'am."

"I still don't know what's really going on here," Lilah stated, "but good people have already died because of this. Whatever's going on out there is behind the situation in Bluth and is probably also behind our livelihood being destroyed. It must be stopped and we are the only ones who can stop it. If I went back to the Directors with this, I'd be laughed out of the room, so we can't depend on anyone but ourselves. And, truthfully, there's no one I'd rather depend on. I've trusted the people of this Hold with my life before, and I'm going to trust them again.

"Brevery, get your fastest ship ready for a trip to Gorsj." He saluted and left the room. "Lieutenant, you have your orders. Get your people ready to train the villagers. And unlock the armory, you'll need to start bonding wands to people today if you're going to have everyone armed in time." Fitzgerald also saluted and left. She turned to me, "Betty..." She stopped.

"I know what you want," I said.

"But, I can't ask it of you," she whispered. "You've done enough and you're hurt." She looked away. "Go home, Betty. I'll let Joshua know how much you've helped."

"And leave you to finish this on your own? Don't be silly."

"You heard the lady!" Jewels interjected. "Let's go.

What more can we do anyway?"

Sam took the words right out of my mouth. "We can infiltrate that base and find out what, exactly, is going on. We can also assess their strength so the ships Lilah hires will know what they are up against and can exploit any weaknesses in the defense. I, for one, would also like to know *why* this is happening."

"Well, I don't," Jewels said firmly. "I'm perfectly happy being ignorant. I've had enough fighting to last me a long time. Plus, I want to live to spend the percentage you still owe me. I think Miss Cat can handle the rest from here." Jewels almost sneered her last words and Lilah's frown deepened.

"She's right, Betty. I don't need your help…"

"Now just stop right there!" I shouted. "That's enough from the both of you. YOU!" I pointed at Jewels. "Her name is Lilah and you will at least use it to her face, regardless of what you say behind her back. You owe her that much respect, at least. And, you aren't getting paid a mark until the job is finished, and, in case you haven't noticed, we're not finished. If you want to sit here and twiddle your thumbs while Sam and I sneak into that port, then, fine. We'll make do without you, but this would be the first time you ever left me high and dry and I didn't think you had any coward in you.

"And YOU!" I turned to Lilah. "Enough with the noble suffering. I know you don't want to ask for my help, but I'm not turning tail and running back to collect my money while you're still sitting here with trouble mounting up. Cristof sent me to help you, and I'm going to do just that. Do you have anything to add?" I looked at Sam.

"No, Betty," he responded while shaking his head, "I think you covered everything." He turned to Jewels. "Let me echo Betty's sentiment. You have never turned your back on us before. You are the best all-around tech I have ever met, and we really need your help."

Jewels glared at both of us. "All right," she said sullenly. "I'll play along. This had better be worth it, Betty."

I glanced over at Lilah, who was biting her lower lip and looking at us with a little more hope in her eyes. I thought about all the harm I had done in my past. I had a lot to make up for and this was a good start. "It's worth more than the money, Jewels. Go get your navy, Lilah. We'll go find out what Harris is doing out there." I looked over at Spanner, "Captain. I'm dependent on you to get us into that port."

He rubbed his jaw, "I can get you near enough. You'll have to take the dinghy in the rest of the way, and you'll have to go in at night. If you're seen and they are hostile, they'll just sink you. I'll let you off a couple islands to the south and then sit at anchor, out of sight until you return."

"If we return."

"Thanks for the optimism, Jewels."

THIRTEEN

I spent the rest of the day practicing walking with the stasis boot. It was a padded metal boot in two halves and hinged. It enclosed my foot with a melded stasis spell to keep any bones from moving. But it also kept me from feeling my foot, was very heavy, and made me extremely clumsy. After an hour of clumping up and down the streets, I grunted in exasperation. "I can't run in this thing; I can barely walk. If I get caught in a line of fire, I'm toast," I complained to Sam, who was helping me.

"You have a tendency to throw yourself into the line of fire, Betty. Your tactics are largely based on being the stronger and faster combatant. This is a good opportunity to adjust to a more strategic battle plan."

"Now you sound like you did when you were my junior instructor at the academy. And isn't it a little late to be changing tactics when we're about to head into a fight?"

"What better motivation to make changes?" Sam asked innocently. "There is, however, a more serious problem. It will be impossible for you to sneak anywhere wearing that boot. You clang like an alarm bell in the city square."

I sighed and stopped, leaning up against the nearest building. "Yeah. I've been using half my brain trying to think my way around that while I was walking. Unless we think of some way to muffle this, stealth is out of the question."

Sam squatted beside me. "Perhaps this is where we return to our original plan," he said. "If stealth is impossible, we try deception."

"You mean I walk in and pretend to switch sides, then you and Jewels pull me out after I've learned their plans?"

"Yes," Sam answered shortly.

"I never really liked that plan, and I certainly don't think it's going to work out there in the middle of the ocean. If we can't just blast our way in, there's no way we're going to blast our way out. And if I'm still in the thick of things once the fur starts flying...that's it!

"What?"

I grinned at Sam maniacally. "We ALL turn ourselves in, get right in the middle of their base, and when Lilah arrives, we start blowing things up from the inside."

"You are talking about a suicide mission."

"I'm not ready to die yet, Sam. We'll fight with them just long enough for them to start to ignore us, then we'll slip away and start sabotaging their operations from inside. I'm sure we can find defensible positions where Jewels can ward us while we break things."

Sam chewed on that for a moment. "First, Betty, you are going to have to convince Jewels to participate."

~

"No! Absolutely I will not!"

Those were just the more repeatable of Jewels's objections to my plan. "I'll go with you to the island and sneak around all you want, but I'm not going to walk right into the dragon's mouth with you."

"All the dragons live up in Durgaland."

"I didn't ask for your input, Samhradh!"

"All right, Jewels. I give." I tried to calm her down. "Just come along as backup to pull my fat out of the fire when it gets too hot."

"With that fat head of yours, that's a big job," she muttered.

I chose to ignore that. "Are you going in with me, Sam?"

"If I stayed with Jewels I would miss all the excitement! Certainly I will go with you. You can look after yourself, Jewels?"

"Oh, whatever will I do without my big, strong, completely non-tech friends to help me?" And she shot an ice spell at the wall to punctuate her statement.

I stared at the shattered crystals mixed with bits of coquina lying on the floor. "Right. While you calm down a little, we'll go start packing."

~

I ran my hand up and down the cool metal shaft of my nature wand. "It's definitely dimming," I told Sam.

"Will it last for this mission?"

"It should. If I were doing this right, I'd recycle it and get a new one, but I don't know where I'd get a replacement around here." I sighed and inserted it into its sheath. "It'll have to do. I just hope it doesn't completely fizzle or, worse, backfire on me."

"Why not ask Lilah for a wand from her armory?"

"They're going to need them for themselves. I'm not going to take one away from them."

"Well, look at it this way," Sam said helpfully, "they will probably take both wands away from you anyway."

"Thanks. I was hoping I'd get them back when the shooting starts."

Sam shrugged his shoulders and continued digging in his bag. "Ah! Here they are. I was beginning to think I had left them behind." He pulled out a pair of sword catchers. "I burnt my staff," he said to my raised eyebrow. "Which reminds me, you still owe me one."

There was a gentle knock at the door and a voice, "It's Lilah."

Sam stepped over and let her in. "Hi," she said as she stepped inside. She was bundled up in a cloak with a hood over her head.

"Are you in hiding?" I asked.

"I've been getting lectures about keeping my priorities straight. I decided I would rather not have anyone in my office know that I came to see you." She glanced over at Sam.

"I am going to go check on Jewels," he said and slipped out the door.

Lilah pulled back her hood and came over and took my hands. "Betty, I...I am so thankful for all your help, but I really hate the idea of you going over to that island—especially in your condition."

"I thought we had already been through this. I'm not going to walk out on you now."

"It wouldn't be walking out!" She was adamant. Dropping my hands, she draped her cloak over a chair and turned away from me. "You've done everything you could be expected to do, and getting your foot crushed...well, no one—least of all me—would blame you for reporting back to Joshua."

I stared at her back, then hobbled over to a chair and sat. "When I first talked with Cristof...he talked about my past. I've never been someone who helped other people. I was just a worker—an enforcer. I did my job, I got paid, I went home and tried not to think about it.

"But...over the years, I have thought about it. About the people I was...'working' on. Were they people who just needed help? And instead of a helping hand they got the back of my hand. Cristof offered me a lot of money to come here...but it wasn't the money that made me take the job. He was giving me a chance to actually be the helping hand. So, yeah, the money was nice, but I didn't come for the money and I'm not going to take the money and run."

While I was talking Lilah turned and looked at me. I stared her straight in the face. "And I'm going to that island not for the money, and not to make me feel better. I'm going there for you. I *am* going to help you, as much as I can."

She came over, knelt in front of me and took my hands again. "What if I don't *want* you to help me that way? I don't want your sacrifice!"

I pulled away, startled at her vehemence. "Whoa. Who said anything about sacrifice? I'm not ready to die yet. Where did you get the idea I was?"

She stood and turned her back to me. "It's just...people have sacrificed for me before. My parents..."

She trailed off. I waited a moment before prodding her. "Is this about how you ended up here? Away from Durgaland?"

"Yes. My parents sacrificed themselves for me to save me and bring me here. Sometimes I wish I had died with them."

"What happened?"

But I had pushed too far and she pulled herself together. "It's not important anymore."

"It is to me."

"No, Betty, what's important right now is finishing this fight with Harris. Are you sure you have to go? You can barely walk. Come with me to Gorsj instead."

"You know I'd just spend the entire time seasick because you can't concentrate on what you have to do while you're babysitting me. And what happens if Harris just chooses to run as soon as your ships show up?"

"So what if he does? He's finished. We know all about his operation out there. What can you accomplish by putting yourself in danger?"

I stood and pulled her hands to me and kissed them. "If I don't go, I'll be lost. Maybe not dead, but I won't ever be able to forgive myself for running, and then what good would I be?"

"You'd be good for me and I would forgive you. But...I understand. I like the man you are and the man you are has to do this." She hugged me and kissed my forehead. Her voice echoed loudly inside my head, "I can *always* hear you." She turned, grabbed her cloak and hurriedly swept out the door.

FOURTEEN

The water below was as black as the night sky above. We had taken our time creeping down along the coast and then up along the chain of islands, spending a good eight days on the cruise to give Lilah time to get to Gorsj and hire ships. Such a long time on the ship gave me a good chance to work on my nausea and I had it at least partially beaten by the time we reached the northern end of the island chain. Sam, Jewels, and I were now in *Sea Lily's* tender slowly running in toward one of the rocky outcroppings south of the suspicious seaport. It was just after sunset, giving us most of the night to scout out the harbor before Sam and I went in.

Jewels was propelling the boat while Sam was kneeling in the prow and directing by pointing his hand. The occasional submerged rock jarred us and once we got caught in a cleft, which we cleared by Sam shifting toward the back so the prow rose up enough for Jewels to back off. After an hour or so of careful maneuvering, we reached a shoaling shore where we beached the boat and crawled forward over a low ridge of sandy rocks.

We were on a southern atoll that formed part of the breakwater for the new harbor. Dark hulks of boats could be seen floating next to piers thrusting out from the shore across the breakwater. To our right the atoll ran into a man-made wall that extended to the other island. To our left was the break through which the ships could enter and leave. On the far shore, lights twinkled in large, blocky buildings.

"Well?" I asked Sam and Jewels.

Sam had pulled a glass borrowed from Captain Spanner and was surveying the harbor. "I believe we can move along the top of the breakwater unobserved. But I cannot see well enough to know what is over there waiting for us."

"Let's get going then," I said and began clumping my way across the rocks as best I could in the metal boot.

"I hope there aren't any guards over there," Jewels said. "They'll hear you coming before we get halfway across."

"This is ridiculous," I said. "If I take this thing off, can you put a stasis spell on my foot?"

"No. I can't do that tech, and even if I could, I can't just put a spell on your foot, and hold it there while doing anything else."

"Just a moment," Sam said. He returned to the boat and dug around until he found a tarp. Using one of his sword catchers, he ripped part of the tarp and came back and wrapped it around the boot. "That will at least muffle it a little bit. Try to put your foot down easily."

"This makes it even harder to walk," I grumped.

"You call that walking?" Jewels clucked at me and then levitated herself over the rocks. Sam and I struggled along in her wake. Once we reached the top of the man-made wall, the surface smoothed out and we could move a little faster. The twin moons were late risers tonight, which helped keep things dark along the wall. With all the light flooding out of the buildings ahead of us, we were counting on the occupants being blind until we were on top of them.

When we reached the wall, Jewels dropped down and walked with us. I noticed she kept digging her fingers into her ears.

"What's the matter?" I whispered to her.

"Bugs! I think," she replied. "Something's buzzing in my ears."

"Jewels, we're out in the middle of the ocean. There are no bugs out here."

"I can hear them," she hissed. "They're buzzing all around my head."

"Stop," said Sam. "We need to figure this out because I cannot hear anything either." We all dropped to the ground as Sam continued. "Jewels, are you sure you are hearing bugs, or are you sensing them?"

Jewels narrowed her eyes at him, and then lost focus as she tried listening with her mind. "Oh!" She let out a little scream and hugged herself.

"Well?" I asked.

"It's the techs. The ones who were controlling the constructs. They're...they're so *loud*."

"Are you shielded?"

"Yes, definitely. Ooooo, I can still feel them, even with shields up." Jewels hugged herself tighter and shivered, though the breezes off the sea were warm.

"How are they doing it?" Jewels just stared at Sam's

question and answered by rolling her eyes.

"Does it matter?" I asked. "Let's keep going and get off this wall before one of the moons comes up and highlights us."

We pushed on and reached the main island without encountering any sentries. The island was a low, sandy mound rising from the ocean and probably no more than a few furlongs long and less than that wide. Large, wooden buildings had been built along the shore and wooden piers stretched into the water as tight as the big ships could be packed in. Rising from the tops of the buildings were large, cone-shaped objects pointing away to the north and west.

Jewels was now visibly shaking and finally dropped and crawled behind a small outcropping of rocks. She started shaking her head, "I can't go on. I can't. I can't."

"Can you listen in to what they're thinking?"

"NO!" Jewels shouted, and Sam and I both shushed her. "They're TOO LOUD. If I tried to listen to them, my brain would explode."

"OK," I said. "You stay here and focus on your shields. Maybe they won't keep it up all night."

Jewels nodded mutely and whimpered and tried to make herself smaller. I pulled the tarp off my boot and wrapped it around her. I knew her shivering was internal, but she hugged the tarp to herself anyway. I turned and looked at Sam. "Ready?"

"After you, sir." He gestured me ahead.

I stumped my way toward the nearest building. "Any idea what's going on in there?"

"I have some vague ideas, but nothing concrete."

"Care to fill me in?"

Sam took in a deep breath. "Magnification? Would that be the proper word? These trollmen were controlling the constructs in Bluth from here, which should be impossible. We arrive here and Jewels is almost immobilized by the magnitude of their thought. They have come up with some way to increase their thought to reach across all those leagues...it certainly is wondrous tech."

"Makes sense. But why?"

"That, Betty, is the two-thousand-mark question, is it not?" We had reached the building and Sam reached out and pounded the door.

"What?!" A voice shouted from inside.

"Inspection!" shouted Sam.

Someone moved around inside and we heard a bolt being drawn. The door started opening and Sam shoved it hard, knocking the man inside back and onto his rear. Sam stooped and strode in, with me hobbling along in his wake. The peon on the floor was disheveled and a little drunk and staring at the towering ogre stooping over him. Another man had half-risen from a table and gaped at both of us. I pulled out my fire wand and pointed it at him. "You just sit there and keep quiet. OK?"

He nodded and slowly sat back down. Sam reached down, grabbed the guy on the floor by the back of his shirt and sat him hard in another chair. "Well, gentlemen," he said, "today is your lucky day. We are not interested in anyone getting hurt. I am sure you can agree with us on that." Both nodded. "Excellent. Now, all we need is to know who is in charge and where we can find him?"

"You're lookin' fer Mr. Harris. And he's right there," the man pointed behind us.

Sam and I slowly turned and raised our hands. Standing in the door was Taylor Harris himself, with an array of soldiers around him.

FIFTEEN

Harris strolled into the room with a couple of guards and hand-motioned us to give over our weapons. I slowly slid my wand into its sheath alongside the nature wand, then slipped the bandolier over my head and held it out. Sam had already reversed his sword-catchers and was holding them out. One of the guards collected them and then we were motioned outside.

"Sir!" A guard saluted Harris. "We've searched the area and seen no sign of the elf."

Harris turned to us, "Where is she?"

I shrugged. "Not here. She didn't want to come with us, so we left her behind." I was hoping we hadn't all been seen crossing the seawall.

Harris glared at me for a moment, then turned and marched off with us being herded in his wake. We passed by a couple of other buildings. All of them were made from the same blueprint by someone who was overly fond of squares and wood. We were finally led into a warehouse—one huge room with stacks of crates scattered about. As we threaded our way through the stacks, I tried to start a conversation. "Nice setup you guys have got here. Do you want to know why we came to visit?"

There was no response. I tried again, "We were hoping to have a nice little chat that could be to our mutual benefit. We know a lot about what's going on."

We were shoved into a small, windowless room. Harris stood in the door and shook his head. "I don't know who you are other than you've been helping the troll, but I'm sure you have nothing I need or even want. Right now, your only use to me is as bargaining chips, so I hope your employer likes you, because if she doesn't..." He shrugged his shoulders and left. The door slammed shut.

The room was completely dark and neither Sam nor I spoke for a while. "Well," I broke the silence, "that wasn't how the plan was supposed to work."

Sam didn't reply and I could hear him shifting and moving around, then he gave a loud grunt and sighed. "What are you doing?" I asked. Still no reply, but he was moving and then I felt his hands groping and he found my hands and untied them and then I untied my feet.

"How do you do that?"

"My thumbs are double-jointed," Sam whispered. "No one ever ties the ropes really tight, so I only have to fold my thumbs inward and I am able to work free of the bonds. Now we need to rely on stealth to achieve our objectives, and there is still the small matter of your special shoe."

"Take it off."

"And ruin your foot?"

"Look, it's going to hurt worse than anything I can imagine, but it's had days in the boot and the bones are probably not going to re-break themselves. So take it off."

"The doctor said you had to keep the boot on for a month..."

"Are you a doctor, Sam?"

"No."

"And you're not my mother either. Take it off."

Sam muttered under his breath, but his hands fumbled with the latches on the boot and it finally came off. With that I lost the stasis spell that had been binding my foot. Fresh fire shot up my leg, and I bit hard on my tongue to keep from screaming. I rode out the waves of pain until they ebbed to a dull ache. "All right," I said. "First, we get out of this room, and second we find our weapons."

"And third?"

"Third, we have a long talk with Harris."

I crawled in the direction in which I thought the door was located, not trusting myself to actually walk on my foot yet. I found a blank wall and decided to go to the right. Around the first corner I found the outline of the door and stopped. I lay on the floor and found the crack at the bottom and placed my ear as near the small opening as I could. After listening for several breaths, I pushed myself up.

"I don't think they left a guard," I said and tried the latch. The door was locked. "Can you force it?" I asked Sam.

"Perhaps, but it might be noisy," he said.

"We'll risk it. Come try."

Sam came up beside me and I rolled out of the way and sat up against the wall. I heard him grunting for a moment and the door creaked. "No good, Betty. The lock is too strong, but I believe the frame around the door is weak. I can probably break it, but that will definitely make a lot of noise."

"Do it."

Sam moved around some more and then his foot hit me in the face. "Ow!"

"Sorry."

"What are you doing waving your feet around."

"I'm getting ready to kick open the door."

"Let me move farther away." I reached out until I felt the corner and then crawled into it. "OK, go."

I could hear Sam taking a deep breath and then the door ripped out of its frame and crashed into the warehouse. I heard a guard cry out. Sam followed his kick out into the warehouse, rolling to a crouch and quickly silenced the guard. I pulled myself to my feet and limped out. There had been one guard outside the room and he had caught the door directly in the back and then Sam had hit him and knocked him out. Sam dragged him into the room where we had been, threw in the pieces of the door, and then went over to a stack of crates. He grabbed one and hefted, but it didn't move.

"Unnh. Betty, come help me, these crates are ridiculously heavy."

I struggled over, wincing at the pain shooting up my leg. I tried to lift, but putting that much pressure on my right foot almost made me pass out. I whimpered and stumbled back, grabbing another stack of crates and standing only on my left foot. Sam looked at me and then at the crate. Finally he set his feet and shoved hard, sliding the crate off the stack where it broke to pieces on the floor.

"Rocks? Why in the world is Harris shipping rocks?" I stared at the pile of rock and dirt lying on the ground.

"Something very strange is going on here." Sam stooped and picked up a rock and walked over to the nearest lamp. He held it near the light and examined it closely for a moment. "Betty, I think this rock contains gold ore."

I limped over and looked it over. It was an average-looking gray rock with streaks and splotches of dull yellow in it. "Are you sure?"

"Not absolutely."

"Well, there's one way to find out. Grab one of those rocks and let's head back to the seawall and see if we can find Jewels."

We crept through the warehouse and peered through a window to see an empty boardwalk outside. Moving as fast as my foot would allow, we left the warehouse and sidled along the walls of the buildings back to where we had left Jewels earlier.

"Jewels? It's Betty and Sam." I whispered.

There was a rustling, and Jewels poked her head up from behind some rocks. The tarp I had given her was draped over her like a cloak. I hobbled over, took off my gold-laced hood, which Harris and his goons had thoughtfully left on me, and put it over her head.

"Ugh, Betty! What're you do…" Her voice trailed off as her eyes widened. "I can't hear them anymore! Actually, I can't hear anything. This is really weird, Betty."

I could barely see her face, because the hood fell so low on her forehead and draped well down her back. "It looks really weird, too," I chuckled. "I'm sorry I didn't think of this earlier, but can you still throw spells even if your 'pathic sense is blocked?"

Jewels concentrated and a small fireball exploded out over the water. "Jewels! They'll see us!"

"Calm down, Betty. It was just a flash. It's a little harder, but, yeah, I can still throw spells."

"Good. Try casting a spell on this rock."

Sam put the rock he was carrying down and Jewels stared at it. Nothing happened. "Go on, Jewels."

"I am! I've thrown three spells directly at it. Is it shielded or something?"

"Something," Sam said. "That confirms it, Betty. Those rocks are gold ore."

"That rock is full of gold?" Jewels demanded.

"Yes," I said, "laced with the only known spell-resistant material in the world."

"And rare," Sam added. "Which only increases its value. But, that warehouse was full of crates. Where did Harris find so much and why is he hiding it out here on these islands?"

"Wait...didn't Lilah's captain say something about ships coming up out of the water?"

"Surely you cannot mean..."

"I know it sounds crazy, but..."

"I'm not keeping up, guys."

I looked down at Jewels. "Harris has found gold at the *bottom* of the ocean."

"You're right, Betty. That's crazy. And why all the secrecy? And those constructs?"

I held up a hand. "We don't have all the answers. The important question is, what now? Do we try to sneak back in and ruin things from the inside, or do we head back to *Sea Lily* and join Lilah's fleet whenever it shows up?"

At that moment, a loud bell began pealing in the harbor and lights began flickering on. We heard yelling and running footsteps.

"The decision has been made for us," Sam said, then he picked me up and began running as fast as he could over the seawall toward the southern part of the harbor. A fireball exploded in front of us, and Sam stumbled as the blast blinded him. Then he slipped and went down hard and I tumbled out over the seawall into the water.

"Betty!" Jewels screamed. I heard shouts and explosions above me, but I couldn't see. I struggled for handholds and began pulling myself when a strong hand gripped the back of my chain and hauled me bodily out of the water. It was an ogre, but not Sam. He was still lying on top of the seawall, on his back with his hands raised up beside his head. Jewels was nearby, curled into a fetal position—the hood had fallen off and the magnified shouting of Harris's techs was overwhelming her again.

The ogre holding me dropped me and I stumbled and almost went down again when my injured foot gave way. With a lot of shouting, Sam was ordered on his feet, Jewels was picked up, and the three of us were herded back toward Harris's secret port.

SIXTEEN

They weren't leaving anything to chance this time. They stripped me of my armor and I was trussed to a chair. Sam was lying nearby, his ankles and wrists in stasis manacles that prevented him even trying to wiggle out, assuming he could wiggle out of metal. Jewels lay next to him, unconscious from a sleep spell. Taylor Harris sat at a table across from me.

Sitting there, leaning forward on his arms, he looked a little like a toad with his round, squashed face sinking into multiple chins that blended directly into his shoulders. He glared at me for a while, then sighed and sat back. The change when he straightened up was palpable and he looked more like a corporate director should look. But the toad image stuck in my head.

"I knew this little operation couldn't run in secret forever, but I was hoping to at least keep it quiet until I ran the troll out of business."

"It hardly seems like a little operation," I said.

He chuckled. It wasn't a nice sound, more like the cough of a predatory animal before it strikes its prey. "You're right about that. I've spent the past five years getting this going. And you and your friends walk in here and blow it up in less than a month." He sighed again, taking in a full tank of air before letting it whoosh out. "So what am I going to do with you, Mr...." He consulted a piece of paper in front of him. "Beatrice Marie Sterling. My, you must have had a lot of fun in school."

"That's one way of putting it. How did you get my full name?"

He tapped his head. "Your elf friend over there was in mental shock. I got one of my 'paths to dig through her brain before putting her to sleep."

"You dirty..."

"Shut up. The troll's got a handful of ogre warships less than a day out and while I could probably handle them, the loss of those warships would not go unnoticed and I prefer to remain unnoticed. I was going to use you as hostages to force the troll to go away. But, well, I think I'd rather have you working for me." He signaled to a man standing off to the side. "This is going to hurt—well, a lot—but I'm absolutely sure you'll forgive me once we're done."

The other man pulled up a chair in front of me and sat almost touching me, leaned forward and grasped my hands, much as Lilah had done when reading my memories.

There are lots of different types of bonding. Spells can be bonded to objects, though we call that 'melding.' Metal works best, but wood or stone are sometimes used. Objects with melded spells are bonded to a person so only that person can use the object. An animal can be bonded to a person and it becomes a slave to its owner; some telepaths like to do that because they can actually 'talk' to their pet.

Bonding a person is a little different. You aren't a slave, exactly, but you tend to go along with whatever your master wants. Parents bond their kids to a bonding agency; it protects them from being forcibly bonded by someone else. My parents bonded me before I was born, which accounts for the unfortunate name mistake.

Force-bonding a person already bonded is hard. You need the person's full name and a fully-conscious subject so you can break down all the psychic barriers between you and their soul. It doesn't happen often and is considered a major crime—almost as bad as murder. And I was about to find out exactly what it was like.

The 'path's mind started whispering in mine. Over and over he repeated my name in a seductive sibilance. Fortunately, I knew something nobody else knew, but I needed to put on a good show. Harris had said this was going to hurt, so I shifted my feet and pressed down hard on my right foot with my left. I gasped and whimpered in pain and tears began streaming from my eyes.

The 'path stared at me and started trying to probe deeper. I resisted the urge to try to block his thoughts and opened up. I felt his thoughts joining with mine and wanted to scream and lash out. Instead, I forced myself to relax and let him rummage around in my consciousness. I slipped into a half doze. After some time, the 'path sat back and looked at me quizzically. "He's all ours, Mr. Harris." But there was a note of doubt in his voice.

Harris peered at me for a moment. "Cut him loose

and give him a knife," he ordered.

"Are you sure?" the 'path asked.

"I'm sure that if you didn't bond him, the first person he'll stab is you. So are *you* sure?"

The 'path swallowed hard, then reached out a hand and a guard handed him a roundel. He sawed at the ropes until they came loose and I pulled my arms from behind my back and rubbed my aching muscles. My new bond-master stood in front of me and held out the roundel—point first. I glared at him until he reversed the blade and handed it to me hilt first.

"Tell him to stab one of his friends," Harris commanded.

The 'path stared at Harris, his eyes wide, then turned to me. "Stab one of them," he said pointing at the prone figures of Sam and Jewels.

I felt the gentle tug in my mind, bidding me do as he asked, but I thought a show of resistance would help, so I clenched my jaw and squinted my eyes and jerked my head back-and-forth. "Do it!" He shouted at me.

Reluctantly, I walked over and knelt beside Sam. We met each other's gaze and he nodded, once. I set the point of the roundel against his chest and then thrust it in, quick and hard. Sam screamed; a loud, shocking sound, and went limp. I stood up, leaving the roundel in his chest, with blood seeping out around it.

The guard who had provided the roundel came over and held his hand out. "Can I have my dagger back?" He looked slightly bored with the whole scene. That's when I struck.

There were three guards in the room, plus Harris

and the 'path. I grabbed the hand of the guard in front of me, and, bending his palm back against his wrist, drove him into one of the other guards. As they collided, I drove the heel of my palm up under the guard's chin, hearing the crunch of bone as his lower jaw ground into his upper. His head snapped back, slamming into the other guard's face and breaking his nose.

I whirled around, getting a quick glance at the room. Harris was bolting out the door, the 'path was screaming at me to stop, and the third guard had produced a wand and was aiming it at me. I grabbed the arm of the guard whose jaw I had just broken and pulled him in front of me. As the spell hit him, I slammed the edge of my hand into the throat of the guard with the broken nose. He choked, gurgled, and went down.

My shield guard was freezing up from the spell fired by the third guard, who was screaming something at me. I wrapped an arm around the throat of my shield, grabbed his belt and heaved him up off his feet and shuffle-charged the guard with the wand. Rather than stand and fight, he fled through the door after Harris, still yelling. I dropped the frozen guard, limped to the door, shut and blocked it.

I turned and looked at the 'path. He had stopped yelling now and was just staring at me. I hobbled over to him and got right in his face. "Wake up the elf," I said. He just stared at me, so I punched him in the gut, doubling him over. "Wake up the elf. Now."

He coughed and nodded, then stumbled over to Jewels and placed a hand on her head. In a few breaths she stirred and moaned. "Good," I told the 'path. "Now sit there and keep quiet." I pointed at the chair where I had been tied. I felt safe turning my back on him; if he had other spells available, he would have used them already.

I knelt beside Sam, who opened his eyes and looked up at me. "Was that really necessary?" he grunted.

"I'm sorry, I wanted them fully complacent before I took them out. I should have only hit muscle."

"Get me out of these manacles and then get this filthy dagger out of me so we can bind up the wound."

I turned to the 'path and motioned him over. "Can you get these manacles off?"

He nodded, still frightened of me, and ran to one of the two downed guards and removed keys from his belt. After a bit of fumbling, he got the manacles off Sam's arms and legs and Sam pulled himself into a sitting position.

"Sit," I said to the 'path, pointing to the chair again. He ran over to the chair and sat down, gripping the bottom with his hands, trying to control his trembling. I went to the non-frozen guard and pulled his tunic and belt off, then got the belt from the frozen guard and went back to Sam.

"This is going to hurt you a lot more than it hurts me," I said. He nodded curtly and I could feel his body tense up. In one quick motion I pulled the roundel free and placed the tunic, well folded, over the sudden flow of yellow blood. While Sam held the cloth in place, I linked the two belts together and tightened them around his chest to hold the makeshift bandage in place.

I turned back to the 'path. "Give me your shirt," I demanded. He pulled it off and handed it to me and I cut it into strips with the roundel. Using the strips I made a sling for Sam's left arm. "You'll have to keep that still or you'll pump more blood out of the wound," I said.

"I know what to do, Betty." He leaned back and shut his eyes.

I looked over at Jewels, who was conscious enough to be rubbing her eyes and trying to sit up. I moved over and helped her up. "How are you doing?"

"I'll be okay," she said.

"Good. How's the noise," I asked, tapping my head.

She shook her head. "They're quiet. I guess they have other things to think about."

"I'm going to question this 'path. Do you want to help?"

Her eyes went flat as she glared at him. I took that as a yes. I went over to the table I had used to block the door, and told the 'path, "Move your chair over here."

As soon as he had his chair pulled up to the table, I placed my hand on the back of his head and slammed it down onto the table. He yelled and sat back up with his head in his hands. "What'd you do that for?" He was crying.

I leaned up against the table. "To keep you from concentrating. If you get tricky, or my friend..." I gestured to Jewels, "tells me you're trying to call someone, I'll do it again. Understood?"

He nodded, still crying. This was going to be easier than I thought. "How long have you been working with Harris?"

"Ten years."

"Then you know everything that's been going on. Lay it out for me. Not the details, just the highlights."

The 'path sucked up some tears and started in. "A few years ago our miners followed a big vein of gold ore right into water. When we checked, we found we were nearing the coast. Our gold mines in the mountains were running out and this looked like a big strike, but we couldn't get to it because of the water.

"Mr. Harris brought in some more techs and we started working on the constructs you saw in Bluth. We were going to use them to mine the gold underwater, but they were too clumsy. We tried making suits that would allow people to breathe underwater, but they didn't work well enough to mine. Then Mr. Harris decided to send some constructs down into the water and just keep blasting to see how far the vein went. It took a couple of months, but we finally broke out into the sea and found the vein actually ran along the bottom of the ocean."

"Are you telling me you're digging gold out there?"

The 'path nodded. "Yeah. We spent a year figuring out how to build a mining ship that could travel underwater."

"What kind of spells let you do that?" Jewels interrupted.

"I don't know, I'm just a 'path. The rest of the tech is beyond me. While other techs were building the ship, we were working on a way to magnify our thought so we could keep constructs working in Bluth."

"Why?" I asked.

"To keep people from finding out what we were doing. The whole setup in Bluth was a decoy, so anybody traveling by would see people working. We even had a Harris construct to help fool people. But we needed to keep them running from out here where the techs were working on the ship, and we couldn't use the tell relays 'cause there are none out here. So we came up with the mega-tells that could send our thought all the way to Bluth and let us control the constructs."

"All this so you can mine some gold?"

"Not just some, Mr. Sterling." The 'path was getting downright polite. He was almost eager to help. "Lots and lots of gold. The vein running through the ocean is huge. Whoever controls that gold would be rich, and it wasn't us because it's not our hold."

"Extraordinarily astute, but, then, he is a businessman." I wasn't even aware Sam was listening. "All the businesses in Ilanerra, as well as other countries, would want to expand their holdings in this area. Indubitably Ms. Burkah would be able to make a claim that all operations in these waters fell under her jurisdiction. She would be quite rich once she finished signing all the mining contracts."

"Yeah," the 'path agreed, "Mr. Harris thought so too. Which is why our mining ship was also being used to catch fish. He wanted to run the troll out of business and buy her out so he could claim the area as his own."

"Betty," Jewels interrupted, "have you got enough? 'Cause if you have, he's been stalling us while they set up an ambush outside."

"Are you listening in?" I asked. She nodded. "Good.

How far along have they got?"

"They're still gathering people and setting up blockades so we can't rush them."

"All right." I turned back to the 'path, who was trembling again. "Thanks for all your help." I slammed his head into the table again, harder this time, knocking him out.

"You enjoyed that," Sam accused.

"I'm a man of simple pleasures." I turned to Jewels. "How much did you pick out of his brain?"

"Lots. He was so busy keeping you busy he never noticed me rummaging around." She gave a snort of contempt. "He wasn't really a very good 'path."

"All the better for us. First, tell me where we can find our equipment."

SEVENTEEN

The room where we had been holed up was small with high ceilings, one door, and no windows. According to the information dug up by Jewels, our weapons and armor were down the hall in another room, but the guards had already set up a blockade between us and that one.

"Is that room on the same side of the hallway as this one?" I asked.

"I think so," Jewels replied. "I didn't exactly get a floor-plan of this place out of him."

I went over and ran a hand down the wall. It was nothing more than thin wood planks tacked onto something. "I wish I had my nature wand," I said. "I could just dissolve the wood and make a hole right into the next room. Can you do that?" I looked at Jewels.

"Nope. Sorry, Betty, fire and ice is all I've got."

"We should not need it," Sam said. He walked over and examined the planks closely. "These walls are not well-built. We could pry some planks off and see what is behind them."

I grabbed the roundel and stuck it in a crack between two planks right next to a nail. I twisted and jerked it back-and-forth until the plank started bending out. Sam and I got our fingers into it and finished pulling it off. Behind we saw it had been nailed to a few posts running floor to ceiling. On the other side were more thin planks making a wall for the other room.

"Let's get more of these off," I said.

Between the three of us we pulled about half the planks off each wall, enough for us to get through, though Sam had to crawl. The room beyond was no bigger, but had a couple of cots and other pieces of furniture. We crossed and began working on the next wall. Outside we could hear people shuffling and whispering and shoving things around.

"Quietly now," I whispered, probably unnecessarily.

We worked at the planks on the wall, trying to be as quick and as quiet as we could.

"I think they're getting impatient," Jewels whispered. "They're planning on charging the room."

"Let them," I replied, "we'll be behind them."

We squeezed into the next room and found my armor and wands and Sam's bracers and sword-catchers lying on one of the cots. While we were suiting up, shouts came from outside and guards stampeded the room where we had been held.

"Where are they!"

"There!"

I turned and looked through the hole in the wall and saw Jewels had already been at work. While Sam and I had been getting suited up, Jewels had built a wall of ice to cover us.

"They'll be in here with us as soon as they get

turned around," I said. "Let's hit them first." I limped over to the door, pulled it open and indiscriminately shot a fireball back down the hall toward the guards. I heard it explode and people screamed.

"This way!" Jewels yelled. She was already off her feet, levitating past me through the door and down the hall away from the guards. I limped along behind her until Sam grabbed me and carried me as we ran from the pursuit.

Jewels took several turns and finally grabbed a door handle, found it unlocked, and flew through. Sam and I followed and she shut the door and froze the handle to lock it.

"Where are we?"

"I don't know," Jewels whispered. "I'm kinda lost. I thought we could hide here until they give up looking."

Sam chuckled.

"They're not going to give up looking, Jewels," I deadpanned. "All right, we're free, for the moment, and armed. What can we do?"

"As much as I dislike the idea, we should split up," Sam said. "If we are individually wreaking havoc, their effort to contain us must necessarily become fragmented. Against small, disorganized groups, each of us would be more effective."

"I don't like the idea either, but I agree with you. What are your targets?" I looked at each.

"I'm going after those tells. I could use one to talk to Miss Cat and maybe even create a little noise for the other 'paths here."

I grimaced at Jewels's using her nickname for Lilah,

but let it pass. "You, Sam?"

"With no tech of my own, I am at a disadvantage in this fight. My best hope is to move swiftly and randomly around the complex and create distractions. It will further disjoint the pursuit."

"I'll take that. I'm going after Harris. I have a strong desire to fold him into a neat little package as a present for Lilah. Jewels, do you have any clue where we are?"

She glared at me and then went glassy-eyed as she probed outward. "There are a couple of guards not far from here. There is a window near them. We could at least see outside."

"Lead us to them."

Jewels warmed up the frozen lock and pulled open the door. She quickly flew down the hall, around the corner and we could hear yelling. She came flying back through the door and landed behind Sam and I who barely had time to set ourselves before two guards barreled through the door. We met each of them with quick gut punches, then Sam knocked them out with the hilt of his sword-catcher.

"I said lead *us* to *them*, not *them* to *us*," I growled at Jewels.

She just grinned at me. "This was quicker." She levitated up and back out and around the corner. Through the complex we could hear shouts as guard units searched for us. We moved as quickly as my lame foot would allow to the window Jewels had found.

We looked out on rocky ground that quickly dipped down into the sea. "We must be at the rear of the complex," Sam said, "opposite the docks."

"Let's get out and get more room to move around," I said. I pulled out my nature wand and described an arc up over the window, dissolving the wood of the wall. As I was coming down toward the ground, my wand sparked and the spell skipped. "Blast! It's dead."

"No matter," said Sam. He set his good shoulder against the side of the window I hadn't finished dissolving and pushed and the section of wall fell outward, splintering at the bottom. I dropped the wand and followed Jewels out into open air.

"Aren't you coming?" I asked Sam.

"That was not my part in this plan," he reminded me. "I will go back in and find things to do. You two run along and have fun." He halfheartedly grinned at us, looking more like a grimace from the pain in his chest, and disappeared back up the hallway.

"Okay, well, have fun chasing Harris," Jewels said. "I'm going up." She pointed toward the roof and levitated up to it.

I looked along the back wall of the complex in both directions. The moons were full and high and their reflection off the water added light to brighten the night. The walls were rough wood and crudely made and stretched several lengths upward. I took off to my left as quickly as I could with my broken foot; I knew it wouldn't take them long to find the huge hole in the back wall and send search parties outside.

I made it to the corner and looked out over the sea. I was on the same side of the island as the breakwater and in the distance I could see what looked like stars moving along the water. Lilah's ships? Probably, but not close enough to make a difference now.

As I turned the corner, heading for the docks, I was knocked off my feet. The roof of the complex had just gone up in a huge explosion that rocked the building. "Jewels," I muttered under my breath. I pulled myself back to my feet and leaned against the building for a moment.

As if our escape hadn't been enough, the explosion had finally brought the entire complex to a state of emergency. I could hear shouting and, through the thin wall of the building behind me, doors banging and feet pounding as they ran. Alarms finally began wailing and lights suddenly flooded the entire island.

I turned and limped off toward the docks. I was near the front of the building when I felt the tingling shock of a spell dissipating against my chain. Berating myself for not moving faster, I pitched forward and rolled, feeling the rocks dig into my arms and back. A pair of guards, both ogres, were standing at the back of the building aiming wands in my direction.

A fire spell hit near where I had just been standing and exploded, singeing my skin. I threw a fire spell back, hitting the building near them and sending them diving for cover. I kept rolling, down off the rocks onto the pebbly strand of 'beach' and into the water. I kept myself in the shallows and pulled myself rapidly with my hands. My armor pulled my body down and I kept just my head above water as I went. The two ogres would certainly be able to see my head in all the light flooding the island, but my hope was they wouldn't be looking in the water until I had gotten into a jumble of rocks near the breakwater.

My luck held. I could hear the guards shouting to

each other in the guttural sounds of Ogrish, but no spells came my way so I assumed they hadn't seen me roll into the water. I got into the rocks, part of a group that had rolled into the water while the breakwater was built. I pulled myself up among them and risked raising my head enough to see what the guards were doing.

They had advanced to the place where I had first been shot and were cautiously picking their way down to the water, looking intently all around them but not far enough down to notice me. I pointed my wand and aimed a fire spell right at one's feet, then immediately ducked down. I heard the explosion and the scream from the guard, and let myself slip further down among the rocks until I was half-submerged again.

There was more yelling in Ogrish, then feet went pounding past me and there was another loud scream followed by the sound of flesh hitting flesh and something fell and splashed into the water of the harbor.

"Is that you down there, Betty?"

"Sam?" I pulled myself back up and saw my ogre friend grinning at me. "Where did you come from?"

"I was hiding in a room with a window that allowed me to see you under attack. I found the nearest exit and arrived just as one of your pursuers was running for help." Sam grimaced and looked at his blood-stained sword-catcher. "I am afraid I had no choice but to take him out with this. Where is the other guard?"

"I hit him with a fireball. I imagine he threw himself in the water to put out the flames."

"In case he survived that, we should vacate the area

soon. Where are you going?"

"If Harris has a ship that can cruise under water, my guess is he's heading for that. I was going to try to get myself on board."

Sam looked back along the harbor at the hulks of ships bobbing at the piers. Dark shapes ran to-and-fro among them, people too busy dealing with emergencies to bother about two distant figures sitting on the breakwater.

"They appear to be making ready all the ships," he said. "How will we know which one is Harris's special boat?"

"Are you coming with me?"

"It was getting far too uncomfortable inside. Besides," he turned to smile at me, "you can barely walk, so someone has to carry you around."

I wanted to make a smart comment about that but decided he was right. "There is that. Okay, pick me up and let's just walk along the pier. I think everyone's too busy to bother with us. Hopefully whatever he's got that mines gold on the bottom of the sea looks a little different than everything else."

Sam put his arm around my waist, hauled me up and trotted along the dock. A few of the people running around glanced at us but who we were just didn't register; their minds were too focused on getting the ships out to sea.

We passed several large, almost block-shaped vessels that we assumed to be cargo ships and then saw something much different. It rode low in the water and the deck was flat with no superstructure of any kind. Sam stopped and put me down and we both stared at the ungainly boat.

"That's got to be it," I said, "but it looks like a floating coffin. Who would get on such a thing?"

"Us," said Sam. He looked around and seeing no one nearby picked me up and jumped over to the deck. He shuffled forward, trying not to pound the deck with his boots, until we found a hatch in the deck. He put me down and hauled on the hatch cover and found it wasn't yet locked into place.

I dropped to my stomach and peered over the edge. Nothing was moving below.

"It's not big enough for you, Sam. I'll go down and you watch my back. Keep anyone from coming in after me."

"Take this," he said, extending his second sword-catcher. "I can only use one arm, so having two does me no good. And you probably don't want to be setting off fires down there with your wand."

"Thanks." I took the sword-catcher, stuck it through my wand sash, sheathed the fire wand, and swung myself down into the bowels of Harris's ship.

EIGHTEEN

A ladder running down a tube gave access to the ship. I went down slowly, setting my feet on each step slowly to avoid noise. Twice I froze as someone walked underneath me, but no one looked up. After hours—well, that's how it felt—of climbing down, I reached the deck. It was nothing but a catwalk running over a deep cargo bay. I was exposed up on the catwalk and needed somewhere to hide, and quickly.

I shuffled down the catwalk hoping no one would come up to investigate or lock down the hatches. Reaching the end, I let myself slide down the ladder, dropping painfully on my feet at the bottom of the bay. Grunting in agony as my right foot hit, I dropped to my hands and knees and crawled in between some crates.

I had just gotten myself settled when voices warned me people were coming. "Cap'n wants everything locked down. We're castin' off." A small group of crew passed and one in charge was giving orders. Two crew climbed to the catwalk to lock down the hatches and two others began securing the pallets of crates.

I wanted to grab one of the crew for the uniform, but the one closest to me was a woman and smaller than me. The guy in charge was about the right size but too far away. I squirmed in further among the crates as the woman came over to strap down the crates I was hiding among.

She shoved one of the crates inward, squeezing me and making me want to yell. I bit my tongue and took it. After pushing against it for a moment, she went over to her boss and complained about something caught among the crates. He told her to forget about it and get the crates strapped down—in slightly more colorful terms.

It took the crew a good quarter hour to get everything secured and then they headed off toward what I thought must be the bow of the ship. The cargo bay went silent until the ship's drive started up and the wood crates clattered against each other.

I crawled out of my hole and surveyed my surroundings. The bay was huge, taking up most of the ship in both length and height. Pallets of crates lined the sides of the bay, leaving the center open. I limped forward, following the direction of the crew. Twice I ducked and crawled behind a stack of crates as other crew ran through. The second time, it was one lone guy.

As he neared me, I stood up, startling him into stopping. He barely got the "Who..." out of his mouth before my fist slammed into his gut followed by a blow to his temple to knock him out. Too bad my injured foot prevented me using kicks; having to punch everybody was cramping my style. I preferred to take them out at the legs first.

I dragged my victim out of sight and pulled off his clothes. They would be a little tight, but I could manage by removing my armor. I hated giving it up, but decided Sam was right—nobody with any sense was going to be blasting spells while under water. Examining the crewman's cap showed there was a thin gold band around the rim; at least my mind would still be protected.

I balled my chain and hood up and used the sword-catcher to bash a hole in a crate and stowed them and my wand inside. I decided to leave the sword-catcher as well and depend on a club carried by the crewman. "Well, if I don't get these back, at least Cristof is paying me enough to buy another set. Assuming I don't go down with the ship." Thus reassured by myself, I tied up and gagged my victim and headed toward the bow.

~

The bow of the ship contained several levels of compartments. I kept my eyes on the floor and shuffled along, trying not to look lost. Other crew hurried past me but never looked at me hard enough to question me. I didn't want to just start opening doors, as I didn't know what I would walk into, so I just kept moving along passageways and climbing ladders, hoping I'd run into something.

That something was the control room. Three levels up and as far forward as I could go, I found a hatch lots of crew were moving through in both directions. I fell in with the press and let myself be washed into a fairly large room fronted by a huge transparent wall. I don't know if it was glass or something else, but beyond was only the dark green of the ocean, faintly illuminated by bright lights beaming out from the ship. Some type of large scoop was positioned just below the level of the window.

Taylor Harris stood at a raised lectern on a platform at the center of the bridge. Around him crew were positioned at panels controlling the ship and just in front was the helmsman. A man who by his dress looked to be the captain stood beside the helmsman.

"Show me the troll's fleet," Harris commanded.

A tech at one of the stations placed his hands on an orb and soon a projection of his mind's eye showed over the glass. I didn't know where he was getting his view, but it was amazingly realistic. It was as if we were skimming just above the waves, rather than under them. Away and to the right could be seen the outline of many huge ships.

"A bit more to port," the captain said and the helmsman responded by turning the wheel over a quarter turn.

"Where are you taking us, Captain?" Harris demanded.

"Begging your pardon sir, but I'm trying to avoid that fleet. I have no idea how much draught those ogre ships carry, but I'm not wanting to bump into one o' them."

Harris wanted to disagree but let it pass. He was staring pensively at the screen when I limped up to him.

"Excuse me, sir."

"What!" He said irritably before turning to me. His eyes went wide. "You..."

I grabbed his wrist and twisted it behind his back while wrapping my other arm around his throat and pivoting on my one good foot to put my back at the lectern. "Yeah, me," I whispered In his ear. "Nobody move!" I shouted for the benefit of the rest of the crew.

It was a ludicrous situation. I was standing in the middle of a room full of enemies, with their boss in a stranglehold, all while on a boat cruising under the water. And, yet, I felt fully in control of the situation. A quick look around at the stunned faces showed me this boat was full of competent sailors and miners but not much else.

"Stop this boat and take it to the surface or I kill your boss!" I twisted Harris's arm harder, making him squeal. He was scrabbling at my arm around his throat with his one free hand, a useless gesture. I added a little pressure to his throat, making his face turn red as he gasped for air.

"Let him go, boy." The voice of the captain came from behind me. "It's a hundred-to-one, you've got nowhere to run, and any one of us can take you out before you have time to do much more than make him blush. Show a little sense, son."

"I'm all out of sense. You want to bet Harris's life on your fighting skill? Bring it on."

I didn't see the captain's command, but he must have signaled because several sailors rushed me. Harris squealed louder and I think he might have been trying to say something, but I wasn't going to let up enough for him to talk. I lashed out with my bad foot against one attacker's knee. His knee crumpled, but my foot screamed at me. For a brief instant my vision dimmed and the world began to swim as I nearly blacked out from the pain. I whirled Harris the other way, so he took a punch that had been aimed at me.

Arms were grabbing me from behind, so I let myself fall backwards, creating a jumbled mess of bodies and pulling Harris down on top of me. I threw Harris off to the side, rolled over and planted a knee on the back of his neck. Kneeling on that one knee, I whipped out my club and made ready to defend myself against the circle of crew surrounding me.

"Stop! Stop!" It came as a wheeze from the figure prone under me. Harris was struggling to push himself up, but he didn't have the strength to get his head moving against my weight pressing it down.

"Let me up, Sterling, and we'll talk." He barely managed to gasp it out.

"Nothing doing. I said it once and I'll say it again. Stop the boat and..."

The boat's drive system suddenly died. It was deadly quiet in the room for just a moment.

"What's happening!" The captain's voice got everyone moving.

"I don't know, sir," one of the station techs replied. "We're getting no response from the propellers. I can't control them, sir!"

"Raise the drive room..."

"Sir!" A tech interrupted. "Drive room is reporting a breach, sir! They're demanding we surface now or we'll sink!"

The captain digested this news then looked at me. "Is this your doing, son?"

I just raised my eyebrows at him. I had no idea what was going on, but I didn't want *him* to know that.

"Bring her up," he sighed.

I kept my knee on Harris's neck as our

windowscape revealed we were rising above the surface of the water. Soon after we were surrounded by the bulks of the ships hired by Lilah.

NINETEEN

I slowly limped along the cargo bay toward the rear of the ship. Orders shouted from the ogre ships made it clear they wanted everyone on deck or they would sink us. Around me dispirited crew were heading for the catwalk and the hatches leading to the deck. As I neared the aft end of the ship, two familiar figures emerged from the drive rooms. I stood and goggled at them as they rushed toward me.

"What are you two doing here?" I was the first to speak.

"Well," said Jewels, "I got to one of those big tells on the roof and contacted Lilah. She got one of her techs to fly her over to the island right away while I had a little fracas with some of the other techs. I think I may have blown a few things up."

"That's an understatement. How did you get in *here*?"

"I arrived in time to see you sneaking aboard the boat." Lilah took up the narrative. "Jewels came down and we decided to come in after you. Once we were on board, though, we thought it would be best if we stopped the engines. So we found the drive room and I threw a shield over the propellers so their techs couldn't control them."

"Uh huh, and while Lilah was shielding the drives, I had a fight with the other techs in the room. I kind of blew a hole in the side of the boat."

I stared at the two of them, then realized something. "'Lilah'?"

"I'm not getting soft, Betty! But she's a really *strong* 'path."

Lilah came over and hugged me then held my face in her hands. "How are you?"

"I'm about to pass out, I feel kind of useless, and why didn't you let me know you were on board?"

"We couldn't hear you," Jewels pouted. "You and that stupid hood. Wait, where's your hood? I still can't hear you!"

"Oh, this." I reached up and took off the cap. "That's better," Jewels's voice sounded in my head. "Yes, much better," Lilah's voice echoed. Then she kissed me.

~

"So, what now?"

Days had passed. We were back in Darfa, gathered together in the one inn big enough for Sam. My foot was once more enclosed in a stasis boot. The doctor wasn't pleased with the regress of my injury and demanded I keep the boot on for at least a half-month. Lilah sat next to me, absently holding my hand.

"There's a lot of debate over who owns whatever gold that's down there in the ocean. But all the gold sitting on that island is mine. We're still trying to assess it, but it will be enough to keep my business profitable for several years."

"Not just your business," Sam added.

"That's right. I've already put a bid in for Harris's Hold and it will probably be accepted. I'll be one of the top Holders in Glomwill." Lilah gloated.

"What about your people? They're fishermen, not miners."

"Harris just about fished the bluefin out of existence." Lilah almost growled as she thought of Harris's aborted plans. "We saved enough to make a start on farming them, but it will take years for them to come back in sufficient numbers." She sighed. "All that gold will help tide us over, though."

"So, everybody's happy?" I asked.

"No," Lilah turned serious. "I'm not happy you're going back to Fisk so soon. You should stay here until your foot heals."

I patted her hand. "I would love to stay, but..."

I trailed off. There was no way to express exactly what I felt. After years spent clubbing people for a few marks, the feeling of helping an entire community deal with its problems felt...well, it felt like atonement. Just like Cristof had said. And there was the little matter of the contract I had signed, the one I hadn't told anyone else about.

I looked at Lilah. "I'll visit. And you should come up to Fisk some time. I'm sure you'd enjoy it. The climate is a lot more like Durgaland than around here."

She shivered. "Thanks, but I've gotten used to not being cold all the time."

~

Two days later we put off for Fisk aboard *Sea Lily*. Tannytown might be the smelliest district in the city, but it was home and it would feel good to be there again. Lilah had ordered a bracelet from Prizm that had the anti-nausea spell melded, so I was really looking forward to the voyage. Maybe this time I could enjoy the scenery.

As the ship pulled out of the harbor, Sam came up beside me. We stood together looking over the prow. "One thing you never explained, Betty. How, exactly, did you resist the bonding Harris's telepath tried on you?"

I stared out to sea for some time before answering. "It was something Cristof did for me when I signed on for this job. He made it clear to me this wasn't just one job, it was a lifetime commitment." I chuckled. "I'm stuck. But, once I signed, he..."

I trailed off and Sam waited a moment before prodding me. "He what?"

"He gave me a new name."

The End

And now, a sneak peek at the next Betty Sterling
novel, "The Prodigal Troll," due June 2014...

THE PRODIGAL TROLL

a Beatrice Sterling novel
by Barry Scott Will

ONE

The distance before me was only a few steps, yet looked like leagues. Where I stood was Fisk, a cosmopolitan mélange of races brought together in common pursuit of wealth and power. Before me stood The Caverns—the troll slums of Fisk.

Trolls built their houses with interconnected upper stories and recessed ground floors leaving the streets as tunnels. Through the tunnel in front of me slouched several trolls—dirt and sweat matting the hair on their bodies, their clothes covered in grime, and gnarled beards covering their faces so all you could see were their eyes. Those eyes glared at me as they passed into Fisk proper, wondering what an outsider could want in their little corner of the city.

I had never entered The Caverns—had never wanted to enter The Caverns—but my current job required it. Mr. Cristof had sent me out to shut down a potion-making ring, and almost a month of investigating had led me here. I pulled out the piece of paper on which I had written directions to a shop and memorized them. I didn't want to act like I was lost or ask for help once I crossed into the slums.

Pocketing the paper, I took a deep breath and strode forward with feigned confidence. The sun disappeared and the air felt as though it were closing in around me. I hadn't gone more than a block when a troll leaning in a doorway stepped out in front of me.

"Where you going, skel?" He growled at me.

"That way," I responded in kind, pointing past him.

We glared at each other. I steeled my eyes and left my hands loose at my side. I didn't want to provoke him by reaching inside my jacket for a wand. He was the first to flinch. He slunk back into the doorway without saying anything, but his eyes never left me. I deliberately turned my back on him and continued on my way.

Signs above the doors advertised businesses, but in Trollish, which I couldn't understand. There were no windows looking out onto the streets, just blank stone walls, interrupted by recessed doors. It really felt like walking underground. My mind flashed back to the trek through the abandoned gold mine down in Darfa months ago, and I wondered what had become of Lilah. After a few tells, she had stopped calling and messages went unanswered. I couldn't get answers out of Mrs. Kyle or Captain Brevery, either.

A passing troll bumped me harder than he needed and I wrenched my mind back to the task at hand. I stopped and got my bearings. I was supposed to go three blocks and turn right. Looking back, I figured I was in the third block and set off to the next cross street and turned right. I started looking at signs until I saw one with the word "Alkym" on it. That was my target.

I pushed open the door and walked into a dingy room lit with an actual candle lantern rather than one with a light ball inside. The room was empty except for a short counter. A troll leaning on the counter stared at me. He had dark hair and wore a vest with a symbol I knew—three eyes arranged inside an inverted triangle. It was the mark of the Treoyn, the potion-runners I was after.

The troll said nothing, so I smiled at him. "I'm looking for some potions," I said.

"Don't you have potion-makers where you live?" he snarled.

"Yeah, but I heard the best potions are made here. I was told to come to your shop specifically."

He grunted. "I don't know who told you that, but if I find out, I might kill him for sending you here. Go away." He turned away.

"C'mon. Give a guy a hand, I really need some of the good stuff."

He whirled around and started to roar at me, "Go awa..." He choked off because I had a wand at his throat.

I leaned in close and stared directly into his widening eyes. "Listen to me and listen good. Two months ago, a woman threw herself off the top of the tallest tower in Fisk. She thought she could fly and she did, but not for long and then she fell—a long, long way down. A few days later, an ogre decided to have some fun by spitting fire from his fingers, then he started breathing fire, then he burned to ash from the inside out. A month ago, a guy walked into a tavern and tried to impress a girl by drinking an enlargement potion.

They're still cleaning bits of him off the walls and ceilings. The girl's getting mental treatment from a 'path.

"Now, you and I know some people think potions are just harmless fun. And maybe the kind that get sold in Fisk proper are just that. They give you some nice dreams, let you levitate feathers, maybe light a candle by blowing on it. But somebody's selling stuff that's a lot more powerful. Too powerful. I've spent a month tracing them down and here I am. And I just want to know one thing."

The troll's eyes had narrowed during my speech. I could see him staring at my wand and I knew what was coming next. There was just the faintest blink as the plan that had been rolling around in his brain went into action. He suddenly threw himself to the side while dropping down, where he probably had wands ready below the counter. Only, he never made it down there. At least, not in good shape.

At the first flinch of the muscles in his shoulder, I folded my arm and slammed my elbow into the side of his face. He went down and I vaulted over the counter and landed on top of him. This time, I put the tip of my wand right under one eye. He almost went cross-eyed trying to see it.

"Now, like I said, I just want to know one thing." I kept my voice even. "Where are you getting your potions?"

His voice trembled as he spoke, but he still had some nerve left in him. "I don't know where it comes from, and, even if I did, I wouldn't tell a skel."

"You think I'm going to believe you don't know

where your own supply comes from?" I pressed the tip of the wand into his cheek right below the eye.

"A runner brings me potions. I don't know who makes them."

"Who's the runner?"

He didn't answer, just glared at me. His trembling was subsiding and I realized I wasn't going to get anywhere with him. I put a hand on his chest and pushed off, standing up with my wand still pointed directly at him. "Thanks for the help. You won't be seeing me again." I backed toward the door as he pulled himself up behind the counter.

I quickly backed to the door, pulled it in, and stepped out, pocketing my wand. I decided to vacate the area of the Alkym shop and walked quickly to the nearest intersection. I leaned against a wall and considered my options.

The shopkeeper was involved; the badge on his vest made that clear. And now the entire ring would know me and know I was onto them. I growled in frustration. I wanted to punch something, but the only productive punching would be to that shopkeeper's face, and that would be too dangerous now. I was going to have to find another place to dig.

I pushed myself away from the wall and right into a troll walking past. I had been so lost in thought, I was oblivious to what was going on around me. We both stumbled and I put my hands out to steady her. Like most troll women, she wore a hooded cape, trying to pass for human. She looked up from under the hood, gasped, and quickly turned and walked swiftly deeper into The Caverns.

My brain was racing, but I found myself following her before my thoughts could settle. She was hurrying along with her head down, pulling her cloak as far around herself as she could. I lengthened my stride to close on her. She turned down cross streets a couple of times and when she finally ducked into a doorway, I was only a few paces behind her.

I shoved open the door and stared at an empty room. Bare wooden walls framed a tiny room no more than a couple lengths on each side. There were no doors other than the one I had just come through and no sign of the troll. The only light came from a lantern hung on the wall next to the door.

I closed the door behind me and carefully ran my hands over the walls. I felt nothing, no faint outline of a hidden door, no concealed latches. Nothing. I sighed and let my head fall back as I leaned against a wall and there it was. The ceiling had a clearly defined trapdoor, but how did she get up through there so fast? And how was I supposed to get up there?

I looked back at the wall framing the door outside. I hadn't examined it before because I was looking for a way in, not a way out. Now I was looking for a way up. I reached out and grasped the lantern and it pulled away from the wall. With a thud, the trapdoor fell open and the upper side had ladder rungs carved into it.

I pulled myself up the door and had my second big shock. The room above me was spacious, light, and airy. Where the streets and lower floors were dank and dark, the walls of this room had many windows opening onto some type of courtyard. Sunlight streamed into the room, illuminating rustic furniture, paintings hung on the walls, and two trolls—a man and a woman—sitting on a divan, staring at me.

I reached down and hauled the trapdoor closed and walked over to the couple and stood there in silence for a moment, staring at the face of the woman I had chased through the streets.

"Hello, Lilah."

Coming June 2014!

Since 2005, Barry Scott Will has written 20 strategy guides for video games across a wide range of genres. His guides have sold several thousand copies and generated more than ten million hits on Web sites such as GameFAQs. His guides have received high praise from readers and won several awards. "A Fine Basket of Fish" is his first novel and introduces readers to a new type of fantasy world, one where using magic is as common as brushing your teeth. Barry currently resides in Virginia with his wife, three children, and ten video game systems.

Personal Web site: barryscottwill.com
Follow on Twitter: @PapaGamer
Like on Facebook: www.facebook.com/PapaGamer66

Read more about Betty Sterling's world at
www.worldofberrea.com